The Mysterious Treasure of the Slimy Sea Cave

#3

The Mysterious Treasure of the Slimy Sea Cave

Rod Randall

Created by Paul Buchanan and Rod Randall

BROADMAN
& HOLMAN
PUBLISHERS

Nashville, Tennessee

© 1999 by Rod Randall
All rights reserved
Printed in the United States of America

0-8054-1000-7

Published by Broadman & Holman Publishers,
Nashville, Tennessee
Editorial Team: Vicki Crumpton, Janis Whipple, Kim Overcash
Typesetting: SL Editorial Services

Dewey Decimal Classification: Fiction
Subject Heading: SKINDIVING—FICTION / BURIED TREASURE—FICTION / CHRISTIAN LIFE—FICTION
Library of Congress Card Catalog Number: 98-37534

All Scripture citation is from the NIV, the New International Version, copyright © 1973, 1978, 1984 by International Bible Society.

Library of Congress Cataloging-in-Publication Data

Randall, Rod, 1962–
    The mysterious treasure of the slimy sea cave / Rod Randall.
        p.   cm. — (Heebie Jeebies : #3)
    Summary: Having explored a sea cave and encountered a snakelike monster covered with green slime, thirteen-year-old Nate finds it coming after him on dry land, prays to God for guidance, and searches for buried treasure.
    ISBN 0-8054-1000-7 (pbk.)
    [1. Monsters—Fiction. 2. Skin diving—Fiction. 3. Buried treasure—Fiction. 4. Christian life—Fiction. 5. Horror stories.] I. Title. II. Series: Heebie Jeebies series : v. 3
PZ7.R158725My   1999
[Fic]—dc21
                                            98-37533
                                                  CIP
                                                   AC

1 2 3 4 5 03 02 01 00 99

Dedication

For Corbin

Chapter 1

Skin diving in the dark? Why me? I must be nuts. Either that or I'm in the mood for night swimming with sharks—which I guess would mean I'm nuts.

As the waves crumble past my snorkel, I try to figure out what brought me here. Then I notice the abalone iron in my right hand. It's a foot long and flat like a small crowbar, the perfect tool for prying. That explains it. I'm hunting abalone, my Gram's favorite food. We can't afford to buy it in the store.

But why at night? Lobsters come out after dark, but not abalone. And why is everything so blurry? I lift my head out of the water and wipe both sides of my mask. Still bad. Nothing is in focus.

Oh well, I'll just have to tough it out. Swimming forward, I hover along the surface of the choppy sea. The flashlight in my left hand slices through the water like a white laser. Moving it from side to side, I eye the bottom of the reef. From above, abalone look like giant clams, with one difference. Clams have two half-shells that close together. Abalone only have half a shell. The open underside has a giant muscle that clings to the rocks, which explains the need for an iron bar to pry them loose. The muscle is what you eat.

Kicking ahead with my fins, I keep watch for my prey. A milky haze hangs in the water just outside the flashlight's beam. Strands of kelp rise from the ocean floor and sway like willow trees in the wind. A few perch swim by, but otherwise the ocean is deserted, almost as if a sea monster has scared everything off.

If I swim just a little farther, I'll be at the cliffs north of town. The water is shallow there and filled with boulders, creating the perfect abalone habitat.

A loud bark catches my attention. Lifting my head, I quickly scan the surrounding sea in the pale moonlight. About fifty feet away, high atop Bride Rock, a sea lion is glaring at me.

He roars again. "What's the problem?" I mumble into my snorkel.

Suddenly a massive wave sloshes around Bride Rock and rolls straight toward me. Gulping down a mouthful of air, I dive deep, waiting for the white

The Mysterious Treasure

wash to tumble overhead.

Caught in the beam from my flashlight, I notice what has to be the world's largest abalone. Clinging to a boulder about fifteen feet below, its shell sparkles like black gold. Talk about buried treasure! The longer I look, the more I have to have it. Rising to the surface, I take several deep breaths and plot my attack. At that depth, I can hold my breath for a minute, max, before having to rise.

I'm hungry, but hesitant. My attack must be quick and precise. I must quickly slip the iron bar underneath the abalone's shell and pop the giant loose. If I don't pull it off in one swift motion, the abalone will get spooked and clamp down tight. Once that happens, I'll never pry it loose.

Doubling over, I position my fins above me and kick like a seal. My heart pounds against my ribs as I descend through the dark and murky water. With my hand just a few inches from the shell, I slide my iron under it and twist. In a flash, my iron pops free. But the abalone is gone! I jab at the rock and barnacles. How could an abalone simply disappear? It doesn't make sense.

My air is running out, but I search desperately, unwilling to give up. My eyes bulge in my dive mask. I have to surface, but something strange is keeping me here—a dark desire to gain the treasure no matter what. I scrape and dig, held down by a new, stubborn greed.

Finally, I concede defeat and attempt to rise. But my abalone iron won't slide free. I yank and heave in a nautical tug-of-war, but the iron bar feels like it is under an elephant's foot. I have to leave it behind. Letting go, I kick for the surface.

Wham!

My head collides with a ceiling of barnacles on a rock that hovers over me. Where did that come from? Swimming beneath the jagged slab, I search for an opening. My lungs want to collapse. My fingers tingle from lack of oxygen. I thrash through the water on the brink of drowning. Suddenly, walls appear on both sides of me, forming a sea cave. The more I swim, the more entombed I become.

Something green slithers past me. I turn just as a serpent's tail disappears into the darkness. I raise my fists in defense, but it doesn't return.

The sea cave begins to shake and rumble as if in the stomach of a volcano. Crabs drop from the rocks, unable to hold on. Kelp are torn from their roots. Debris and sand cloud the water. I can't see anything, and I can't hold my breath any longer.

I feel like I'm in a blender. I can't fight it any-

The Mysterious Treasure

more and begin to black out. My lungs are ready to burst and take my heart with them. The rumbling intensifies.

Then something grabs my arm. It must be the serpent, back to chomp me to pieces.

"Nate!" a voice calls.

The turbulence around me continues.

"Nate!" the voice repeats, sounding more familiar. "Wake up!"

The outline of a woman's face peers down at me. It's Gram. But she doesn't go skin diving. What's going on?

"Get up! Quick!" She hollers, pulling me by the arm. "It's an earthquake!"

Sitting up in bed, I realize what has happened. I've gone from one nightmare to another. But this one is real. The sea cave doesn't exist, but the earthquake does, and our old house is about to come crashing down.

Tossing my covers aside, I scrambled under my desk. Gram made her way to the door frame and stood under it.

"Where's Paige?" I asked.

"What?" Gram hollered, unable to hear me over the rumbling.

This time I yelled. "I said, where's Paige?"

"She's already under her desk. She's fine."

As the earthquake intensified, I wondered whether our house would survive. The windows rattled almost to the point of shattering. Pictures on the walls swung like pendulums. The crash of glass breaking echoed from the kitchen.

Closing my eyes, I prayed for God to keep us safe. I also asked Him to watch over our house. I knew Gram didn't have earthquake insurance, or, for that matter, any money for repairs.

Huddling under my desk, I marvelled at the night's events. To have such a vivid and eerie dream followed by a real earthquake was too bizarre to be a coincidence. As the shaking subsided, I tried to make sense of it all; but nothing I imagined came close to what would soon unfold in the wake of this ominous night.

Chapter 2

The next morning Paige and I helped Gram clean up. Miraculously, the tremor had only broken two glasses, so it didn't take long. I checked outside and found no further damage. We all exhaled in relief.

"Looks like God answered my prayer," I said.

"He always does," Gram added with a smile. She has blonde hair with a touch of gray. People always say she looks too young to be a grandma.

Following a quick cereal breakfast, I headed for the phone to call Zack, my best friend. He's in ninth grade like I am and always ready for an adventure. But as I reached for the receiver, I hesitated. After last night's dream, I wasn't as excited about our plans to go skin diving. Then again, that was only a dream. There isn't a sea cave anywhere near Starboard, which is where I live.

Finally, the thought of abalone for dinner was too tempting to pass up. I picked up the phone and dialed Zack's number.

"How's the house, Dude?" he asked me right away.

"A few glasses broke, but that's it," I told him.

"Same here."

"So are you ready?" I asked, eager to change the subject.

"For what?"

"Skin diving. It's ocean time."

"Not for me. I've got plans to go treasure hunting."

If treasure hunting meant searching for buried treasure in the sea, I would jump at the chance to go along. But it doesn't. For Zack, treasure hunting means garage sales. He collects artifacts and antiques related to the ocean. Because some of the houses in Starboard are over 100 years old, garage sales provide the best and most affordable way to feed his addiction. Some of his finds include a harpoon, a pirate's sword, a brass bell, a compass, a cannon ball, and a captain's log dating from the 1880s. He has lots of other stuff too, some of which is kind of cool, but hardly worth living for.

"How do you know if there are any garage sales today?" I asked, hoping to persuade him to come along.

The Mysterious Treasure

"My mom saw a sign when she went for her morning walk. Let's skin dive when I get back."

"The water will be choppy by then. Why don't you hit the garage sale later?"

Zack snorted. "All the good stuff will be gone. You know that."

I did but figured it was worth a try. When neither of us would give in, we agreed to go our separate ways.

"I'll go with you," Paige called from the other room.

Before I could answer, she came clomping around the corner, already decked out in her bright pink wetsuit with matching fins, snorkel, and mask. Her long, blonde hair was pulled back in a ponytail. At eleven years old, Paige is small for her age, but that doesn't hamper her ability in the ocean. My sister not only looks like a mermaid, she swims like one.

"I'll go with you," she repeated.

"Nah, that's ok," I said, feeling some relief that it wasn't going to work out. As hard as I tried, I just couldn't get the sea cave nightmare out of my mind.

"Come on," Paige persisted. "You know how much an abalone dinner would mean to Gram, especially after losing two glasses and her favorite vase."

Heebie Jeebies

"Her favorite vase?"

Paige nodded. "All it did was fall over, but that was enough to crack the crystal."

I felt terrible because I knew that the vase could not be replaced. What little money Gram earns goes to supporting Paige and me. When I was three and Paige was one, our parents died at sea during a storm that capsized their boat. Gram was our only living relative, so we came to stay with her. Even though we cramp her living space and she has to give up so much of what she enjoys, she never complains. Instead, she carries on about how blessed she is to raise us as her own.

"You're sure you want to go?" I asked, stalling. "The earthquake might have churned up the water pretty good. Maybe some kind of slimy sea monster was released from the deep."

Paige scrunched her eyebrows together. "Yeah, sure. A sea monster. Let's go."

I watched as Gram carefully laid the vase in the trash and closed the lid. Keeping her face hidden from us, she walked down the hall to her bedroom. That was enough for me.

"All right," I said. "Let's go catch some dinner for Gram." As the words crossed my lips, all I could think about was the green tail of a serpent wrapped around my throat and holding me down.

Chapter 3

I was right about the earthquake's effect on the water. When we got to the beach, the bay looked like a backed-up sink. Underwater the visibility was six feet at best. Some sections were so bad, it seemed like we were swimming at night. Keeping an eye on Paige was nearly impossible. Not that she needs my supervision. Having grown up near the ocean, she can swim circles around most divers, adults included.

Because of the low tide, more rocks than usual protruded into the open air, making our surface swim a little tricky, especially with the strong surf. At times it felt like we were in some kind of aquatic maze. After a lot of kicking and paddling, we navigated our way to the cliffs north of Starboard.

Fortunately, as we swam, the visibility gradually improved. No sooner had we reached the cliffs than

Heebie Jeebies

Paige spotted and bagged an abalone in one swift motion. The shell was seven inches across, easily big enough to feed Gram.

"It's no sea monster," Paige teased. "But it will do."

"Funny," I said, not in a mood for joking.

Moving along the cliff, I noticed a massive abalone in about twelve feet of water. Gripping my abalone iron, I reminded myself that last night's dream was just that, a dream.

"This is reality," I whispered into my snorkel. "And I'm going down."

But even as I dove, I found myself checking to make sure an overhang hadn't quietly drifted above me.

All clear.

As I reached the bottom, the cold ocean pinched my head like a vice. As quickly as I could, I sprung the abalone loose from the rock and tucked it into my dive bag. Returning to the surface, I purged the water from my snorkel and breathed deeply. What a relief! The dream wasn't a foreshadow of doom after all. I glanced at the abalone in my bag. It was at least eight inches across, which was more than enough to feed both Paige and me. Amazing.

Now we could relax and enjoy the dive. If we found more abalone, great, but it wasn't necessary.

The Mysterious Treasure

The white wash from a wave cascaded over my head like an avalanche, but I didn't mind. Things were looking up.

Or so I thought.

"Yeow!"

Something jerked my foot and pulled me under! I thrashed at the water, determined to get away. Twisting free, I rocketed to the surface and gulped some air. *Something is down there!* Paddling away, I searched through the water.

Two eyes stared back at me, followed by a smile from ear to ear. It was Paige, playing a practical joke. I was tempted to bag her like an abalone, except instead of taking her home, I would leave her for the sharks.

"Someone's feeling jumpy today," she giggled, joining me on the surface.

"Don't you ever—" Something at the shoreline caught my attention; something I had never seen before.

Paige noticed my intense expression and said, "What's wrong?"

I ignored her, transfixed on a dark opening in the cliff. A sea cave, the size of a whale's mouth, swallowed the surf that washed into it. Sharp rocks and barnacles lined the edge like teeth. No matter how many waves washed into the cave, it continued to gulp them down.

"A sea cave?" I gasped. My fingers and toes tingled with adrenaline. I swam over to take a closer look, but I was dreading it at the same time. Most of the cave lay below the surface, but a small part of the opening was above the water. *Talk about weird. Of all the times I've gone skin diving here before, I've never noticed this cave.*

"Is that what I think it is?" Paige asked, following in my wake.

I nodded. "And the location doesn't thrill me either."

Paige and I stared at the top of the cliff directly above the cave. A massive three-story mansion hung over the edge like a vulture. Old Man Ingram's place, where he lives in dark solitude. The building's stone walls looked heavy enough to crush the ledge and plunge the whole structure into the sea.

"Right below the Ingram estate. How nice," Paige said sarcastically.

"Tell me about it. If a house is haunted, the cave beneath it must be—"

"There's only one way to find out," Paige interrupted. "Let's have a look."

As Paige headed for the opening, I grabbed her by the ankle. "Slow down," I cautioned. "You don't

The Mysterious Treasure

know what's in there, or how far back that air pocket goes. What if you get stuck underwater?"

"Stuck? I'm only going in a few feet. I can always swim back out."

I shook my head. "Not if the waves are crashing against you."

"Are you saying you don't want to check it out? *You?* Mr. Sea Stud, himself?"

"Well, when you put it that way," I said, lowering my manly voice, "maybe we should have a quick look. But I'll lead."

Treading water, I paused to clear my mask. With so much of my dream coming true, I wondered how long it would be until my mask went blurry. Or worse yet, how long until I tried to surface and conked into a submersed slab of solid rock.

Paige followed me as I approached the mouth of the cave. With the waves breaking over us, we had to repeatedly dive down, then rise to clear our snorkels. Just before going inside we turned on our dive flashlights. Even though it was daytime, we always brought them along for searching under rocks.

The cave appeared to go about twenty feet back before the ceiling sloped into the water and put an end to the air pocket. We couldn't tell whether the cave ended there or continued into the cliff entirely below the surface. With the poor visibility, we would have to swim there to find out.

"Ready?" I asked.

Paige nodded, and we swam into the cave, flashlights in hand. The visibility improved with each kick of our fins. As we approached the middle of the air pocket, the waves died down and we were able to enjoy an array of sea life. The cave walls were lined with mussels, sea anemone, and starfish. Several crabs and a few lobsters scuttled into view on the ocean floor. "Too bad they're out of season. I don't see any abalone."

We reached the end of the air space that lined the top of the cave. "Now what?" Paige asked.

Pulling my mask from my face, I drained some water that had leaked in. "We should probably go back," I told her. But in my heart that's not what I wanted, and she knew it.

"If you want to go a little further, I'll wait here," she suggested.

The more I searched toward the back of the cave, the more Paige could tell I didn't want to give up. And neither did she.

With my face submerged, I stared into the liquid darkness. The cave went back another ten feet at least. I could easily swim that far and back on one breath, but my dream kept coming to mind. I never

The Mysterious Treasure

wanted to do something and *not* do something so much in my entire life. But I couldn't be superstitious. And I couldn't let Paige check it out first. I'm the stronger and more experienced swimmer. If anyone was going deeper into the cave, it had to be me.

I took several long breaths through my snorkel, then lunged forward into the sea cave. The walls were rough and dark, like a freighter's smoke stack buried at sea and covered with rust. I swam ten feet, then twenty. That's when I noticed my light reflecting on the top of the cave. It looked like an air pocket. It was still a ways ahead, but grew larger and larger the closer it got. My lungs began to squeeze, but I had to find out what lay ahead.

Poking my head up, I gasped in awe. The sea cave ended in a cavern the size of a small garage. A five-foot stretch of beach separated the water from the back stone wall. I swam forward and clambered onto a rock. The air was damp and stale, but seemed safe to breathe. Shining my light around, I could see that the ceiling came together in the form of a chute that rose high into the cliff.

I was about to try climbing when something bumped my submerged ankle. I flinched, but remembering my last episode with Paige, I quickly calmed down.

"Funny, Sis," I said, shining my light into the black water. But the beam just bounced off the surface to the opposite wall. Paige was nowhere to be found. I shined my light all around, but I couldn't see a thing.

The incoming tide swiped my feet, and I lost my balance. I tried to steady myself, but as soon as I grabbed onto a rock, I let go, grossed out by its squishy surface.

A blob of oozing green slime dripped from my hands.

"Yuck," I complained, washing it off. As I did, another bump hit my leg. This time I jumped right out of my fins and onto the beach.

Chapter 4

A moment later Paige surfaced. "Nate, you've got to calm down," she teased. "You can't be *that* afraid of me."

"It's not you I'm afraid of," I told her.

"But you *are* afraid," she smirked, with a coy expression.

Seeing no other way around it, I told her about last night's dream.

Paige's mouth dropped open. "No wonder you're so freaked out. If I had that dream, I wouldn't come anywhere near the ocean today. But I'm glad we did. This place rules."

"That's for sure," I said. "The only hard part is getting used to this slime."

"What slime?"

When I pointed it out, Paige made a face like she had just seen a monster. For the next ten minutes we examined the cavern, trying to avoid the splats of slime. My interest was in the narrow chute above us. It rose like a watchtower from an old castle. Then, about thirty feet up, it just stopped. I shined my light all around, trying to see what was up there. Paige waded back to the mouth of the cavern to get a better look.

"Too weird," I muttered, expecting Paige to agree.

But she didn't even acknowledge my comment.

"Paige?" My light and eyes were still fixed on the ceiling.

No response.

Returning my attention below, my eyes met Paige's as she let out a soft cry.

"My foot's stuck," she said, her face twisted with pain. "I tried pulling it free, but it won't come loose."

She held her fins in one hand and her flashlight in the other. The sea swirled past her shoulders, then subsided again. After giving her every piece of advice I could think of, I didn't know what to do.

Suddenly, the walls looked like they were moving. I rubbed my eyes and realized that the rock wasn't moving, but an army of crabs was converging on Paige like wolves.

The Mysterious Treasure

"We've got to bail . . . now!" I ordered. Moving toward her, I yanked her leg, determined to free her.

"Ouch," she yelled. "You're hurting me."

Crabs closed in, their pinchers seemed large enough to snap a bone. Using my fin, I flung the closest one away. Ten more took its place, as if ready to enjoy the spoils of their human trap.

"There's no way to fight them all," I cried.

Several disappeared into the water. They fanned out to surround our thighs and ankles. I braced myself for their claws.

Paige screamed out as one crawled over her shoulder. Before I could bat it away, it kept going, as if Paige was nothing more than a stepping stone. I watched, too stunned to move, as more and more crabs sped past us. *What's the rush?* I wondered. *Is the serpent back? Mr. Maker-of-Slime himself?*

I lowered my mask into the water, searching for his long, slivery form. With Paige stuck, I vowed to use my abalone iron to defend her. I would lay down my life, if need be, to fight the serpent.

But the mysterious sea monster was nowhere to be found. I shined my light in every crevice, but all I could see were crabs by the dozen, darting through the water heading for the cave's opening.

"This is too weird," Paige said, watching the crabs glide past.

"Yeah, it is," I responded, still mystified.

With the next surge, I figured out what was happening. Water splashed over Paige's head, leaving a crest of white foam on her blonde hair. The tide was coming in . . . and fast! That's why the crabs were leaving, to find a better place to wait out the rising surf.

From what I could tell, we had about five minutes to swim to safety. As another wave sloshed over Paige's face, she donned her mask and snorkel. I quickly did the same and dropped down to have a closer look at her foot. The rocks angled together on one side, but on the other they opened slightly. *There's only one way out.*

I surfaced to explain my plan, but it was too late. The rising tide had buried Paige's face completely. If not for her snorkel, she'd be gone in less than a minute. Diving back down, I grabbed her ankle and pushed it toward the open side. Paige resisted and water clouded with blood. The barnacles on the rocks were cutting into her skin.

Grabbing another breath, I dove again, determined to free her foot, but knowing that if necessary, I'd rather she lost her foot than her life.

This time I shoved her ankle toward the opening as hard as I could. Blood wafted through the water like red smoke. Just as my breath was about

The Mysterious Treasure

to give out, Paige's ankle came free.

Still in the cavern, we surfaced to the small beach to make sure Paige was ok. Parallel cuts, as if made by a tiger's claw, wrapped around her ankle.

"Cool pattern," I joked, trying to cheer her up. "How does it feel?"

"Just peachy," she replied dryly.

"You know what I mean. Can you swim with it?"

"No problem. They're just surface cuts."

"Ok. I'll follow you out. But we've got to hurry," I said urgently. "It's probably forty feet to the opening of the cave by now. And that's against the tide."

Soon an outgoing surge of water retreated through the sea cave. Taking one last breath at the edge of the cavern, we swam along with it. Diving into the submerged section of tunnel, we thrust wildly for daylight at the other end.

Paige's fins stroked the water just in front of my mask. Still more crabs lined the walls, scampering for the opening. I held my flashlight with one hand and felt my way with the other. The incoming tide brought in clouds of loose debris and bubbles, making it hard to see.

With so many barnacles lining the walls, we might as well have been swimming through a giant cheese grater. I did my best to avoid the sharp surfaces, but my arm scraped just long enough to tear the skin, sending a trail of blood past my mask. Between Paige and me, the sea cave was about to become a shark smorgasbord.

Suddenly, Paige's fins were in my face. Her strength had given out with at least twenty feet left to swim. My lungs throbbed for air, and I knew hers must be doing the same. Grabbing Paige's foot, I shoved her forward. Unfortunately, that pushed me back and up. The incoming surge made things worse. Closing my eyes, I prepared for the sharp grating of my head on the roof of the cave.

My head bumped against a solid surface, but instead of being sharp and cutting, it felt smooth and slippery. Working my way forward, I rolled over to see what I had bumped.

If it were possible to scream under water, I would have let loose. Two fierce eyes stared back at me, above a set of jaws large enough to swallow me whole. Rolling back over, I swam for my life. Ten feet more. Five feet. My hands and feet thrashed the water in terror. Reaching Paige, I grabbed her arm. We launched from the tunnel together and exploded to the surface.

Paige wanted to pause and celebrate, but I wouldn't let her. I led the way as we sped across the surf. We dodged rocks and ducked under waves

The Mysterious Treasure

until we reached the bay at the end of the cliffs.

Climbing out of the water, I described to Paige what I saw, and *felt,* in the cave. At first she didn't believe me, and she squeezed the back of my hair for proof.

"Gross!" she squealed.

"What? What is it?"

Without a word, she extended her hand, which was dripping with green slime.

Chapter 5

On the walk home, I tried to calm down and get my mind off of the giant serpent that practically swallowed me for brunch. Walking through Starboard helped. It is a picturesque sea town with lots of quaint buildings of wood and stone. The park benches are made of polished driftwood. Wind chimes made of shells hang from every house. Flowers grow thicker than weeds, blooming from window boxes, gardens, and even cracks in the sidewalk.

"How's the ankle?" I asked Paige.

"Better. The cuts aren't as bad as they first looked. I'm fine."

"I was hoping you'd say that. Do you mind going home to clean the abalone, while I stop off at Zack's?"

"Not a problem," Paige said. "I can't wait to see the expression on Gram's face."

I handed her my dive bag. "These won't make up for the broken vase, but they'll help. Just don't tell Gram about the sea cave—at least not until I'm there. She'll probably freak and tell us not to go back, especially when she learns it's under Old Man Ingram's."

I turned at the corner and headed for Zack's. He lives a block over from us but in a much larger house. His room is twice the size of mine and loaded with collectibles.

As I knocked on the door, I wondered what treasures he found at the garage sales. *Is he even home?* No one responded, so I knocked louder. The door swung open, but no one was there.

"Strange stuff," I mumbled under my breath.

When it comes to locking the front door, Zack is usually even more diligent than his parents. He thinks that thieves are continually prowling the streets waiting for a chance to break in and steal his nautical antiques. I've tried telling him it's just old corroded junk, but he won't listen.

"Zack?" No answer. I decided to try calling his parents. "Mr. Hayes? Mrs. Hayes?" Glancing out front, I noticed the cars were gone.

Hesitantly, I decided to go upstairs to Zack's

The Mysterious Treasure

room. *Maybe he has his headphones on and the stereo cranked.* But at the top of the stairs, I could see that his room was empty. *Well, he's not there.* But with all the maps, model ships in bottles, sailor's coats and more, his room was never empty.

With Zack out somewhere, I decided to leave. As I turned to head for the door, something poked my back.

"Yeow," I yelled, jumping into Zack's room. Before I landed, I heard him laughing behind me.

"Where were you?" I asked, trying to relax.

"In my parents' bedroom," he laughed. "You must have had a wild time in the ocean. Either that or you're still freaked out about the earthquake."

"Both are true and then some." I filled him in on everything that had happened to me, from last night's dream right up until the end of the dive. At the mention of the sea cave, Zack's eyes nearly popped from their sockets.

"I don't believe it!" he gasped. "And neither will you." He leaped to his feet and ran to his parents' bedroom, returning with something hidden behind his back. "Guess where the garage sale was this morning?"

I shrugged.

"The Ingram mansion."

"Get serious," I scoffed.

Heebie Jeebies

"I am serious. At first I couldn't believe it either," Zack said.

"Did you get a look inside his house?" I asked, curious to know what it looked like. Old Man Ingram lives alone and never ventures outside. His groceries are delivered by the local market. Ten foot iron gates keep everyone else away.

"Not one peek," Zack conceded. "Everything was piled on the driveway. Even the garage door was closed."

"At least you got inside the gates," I said. "Now let's see what you got."

"Check it out," Zack said as he held out a spyglass, complete with brass trim. It looked like something a pirate might carry to search for Treasure Island. "That's why I was in my parents' bedroom. I was watching boats on the ocean."

"I still can't believe Ingram had a garage sale—and on the same day we found a cave beneath his house. What'd he look like anyway?"

"Creepy, but not as bad as I thought he would. He has one of those sea captain's beards and the thickest white eyebrows you've ever seen."

"What about his teeth? Were they as sharp as a shark's, like people say?"

"Beats me. He never smiled. The only time he even spoke was when someone asked him a

The Mysterious Treasure

question about his stuff," Zack said, scratching his head. "Except in my case."

"What do you mean?"

"When I first looked through a box of stuff, the spyglass wasn't there. All he had for sale was a bunch of old clothes. But when I came back for another look, the spyglass suddenly appeared. The second I picked it up, he asked me what I would pay for it."

"What'd you say?"

Zack let out a laugh. "I told him twenty bucks, as a joke. I knew it was worth ten times that."

"Did he get mad?" I asked.

"That's the weirdest part. Not only did he *not* get mad but he held out his hand and said, 'deal.' Can you believe it? I slapped down a twenty and got out of there as fast as I could, before he changed his mind."

"Unbelievable," I marveled. Taking the spyglass from Zack, I searched the horizon outside the window. The magnification was at least twenty times, like a high-powered pair of binoculars. No wonder Zack was so keyed up; this thing was worth a fortune.

While it was hard not to be happy for Zack, what I couldn't figure out was why Ingram made the spyglass available. Zack grabbed the spyglass back and placed it carefully on his shelf. He sat down on his bed and looked proudly at his many treasures.

My excitement for him quickly dissipated. The more I watched him revel in his possessions, the worse I felt. It's not that I have anything against maps, or brass bells, or harpoons. What bothers me is that Zack is so wrapped up in all his things. Sometimes it seems like they are all he cares about.

I know Jesus said that where your treasure is, there will your heart be also. Looking at Zack's nautical antiques was like looking at his heart, and that was depressing.

Time and again I had asked him to go to church with me. But he always declined because of potential garage sales. He said he was afraid he might miss out on some priceless treasure. He is missing out on a priceless treasure, but it has nothing to do with garage sale antiques.

"I say we head back to the tunnel first thing in the morning, when the tide is low," Zack announced.

"How about first thing next year," I said.

"Get serious. You found the ultimate treasure hunter's dream. We can't just ignore it."

"You heard what I said about the serpent and slime."

The Mysterious Treasure

Zack rolled his eyes. "Serpent? Green slime? Get serious. The serpent was probably a moray eel. The slime must have been from a sea anemone." He just shook his head. "If I have to, I can go alone. But since you found—"

"You're not going alone," I cut in, dreading the consequences if he did. "Skin diving alone is never safe. The sea cave would only heighten the danger. I'll go, but we're getting in and out before the tide rises."

"Unless," he protested, raising his hands. "We're too busy digging up gold and jewels to notice."

When I shook my head in disgust, Zack quickly added, "I'm just kidding. Your plan sounds great."

I offered a hesitant but willing smile. Of all the words I could use to describe the sea cave, *great* would not be near the top. And something told me that after tomorrow's visit, *great* wouldn't even make the list.

Chapter 6

Gram loved the abalone and wanted to hear again and again where we found them, which didn't surprise me. Abalone have gotten pretty scarce in our area.

It's a good thing we didn't find them in the sea cave; otherwise all of Gram's questions would have pulled the information out of us by now. I could tell that Paige was dying to tell Gram all about our adventure; but with dinner nearly over, she had somehow managed to keep quiet about the cave. I intended to keep it that way by bringing up Zack's find at the garage sale.

"Gram, what do you think an antique spyglass would be worth?" I asked.

She pursed her lips and eyed me closely. "If it's in good shape—and a real antique—I suspect a few hundred dollars or more. Why?"

Heebie Jeebies

"Zack got one today for twenty bucks."

"Really?" Gram stopped chewing her abalone, and leaned forward. "Where?"

"A garage sale," I said casually, after taking a drink.

Gram rested her fork on her plate, no longer interested in her food. "At whose house, might I ask?"

"It wasn't at a house," I said, hesitating, suddenly uncomfortable with where this was going. But I broached the subject and couldn't shut down the details now. "It was a mansion, Old Man Ingram's."

"Mr. Ingram's?" Gram choked. She looked at me as if *I* had done something wrong.

Not sure of what to say, I picked at my rice, stabbing individual pieces with my fork. Ever since we were young, our negative impression of Old Man Ingram had come primarily from Gram. It's not that she slandered him, or accused him of some unspeakable horror. She just made it clear that he was to be avoided, as if a contagious evil clung to his skin and would quickly spread to those who drew near.

"Mr. Ingram never comes outside," Gram said, still glaring at me.

The Mysterious Treasure

"I know. Zack was in shock." I explained to her everything Zack told me.

"What else did he have for sale?" Gram wanted to know.

"Mostly clothes, I guess. And a few old tools."

Gram held still for a moment without even blinking, then forced a smile, as if to convince us that everything was fine.

But I could tell that things weren't fine, and I wondered what was going on. It was a good thing we avoided mentioning the sea cave. That might have really freaked Gram out. At least I thought we had avoided it . . .

"So Zack went to Ingram's too?" Paige blurted out.

I stabbed Paige with my eyes, hoping she'd pipe down. But it was too late.

"What do you mean by that?" Gram asked, directing her attention to Paige.

Paige looked at me with fear in her eyes.

Shaking my head, I reviewed everything that happened to us on the dive, including the cave discovery and Paige getting her ankle stuck.

Gram let me finish, then expressed her disappointment. "You should have told me right off. How can I trust you if you keep secrets from me?"

"It's just that we wanted to go back," I explained. "We didn't think you'd let us if you found out where it was."

"You're right about that, young man," Gram snapped. "Consider today your first and last visit to that sea tomb."

I dropped my eyebrows, confused. "Actually, it was a cave. And what's going to happen to Zack if we don't go?"

"What's Zack got to do with this?" Gram fumed.

"He says he's going no matter what. You know how crazy he is about treasure. He can't wait to search the cave. Besides, nothing is going to happen to us. We're safer in the water than out of it. You know that."

Gram appraised us both, then clasped her wrinkled hands against her forehead as if in prayer. When she spoke, she didn't look at Paige or me. "All right. But no matter how tempting something seems, don't risk your life for it."

Gram's words stuck in my mind. It would have been much easier to just say, "Be safe." *She knows something about the sea cave that we don't.* I was about to ask, when a loud boom rattled the windows.

"What was that?" Paige asked. She jumped up and opened the back door. A solid downpour

The Mysterious Treasure

greeted her. The rain was so heavy it looked like water cables hung from heaven to earth.

"Lord, have mercy," Gram whimpered.

"Why are you so worried?" Paige asked. "We could use a good rain."

"The earthquake," Gram answered. "When you kids were gone I had a closer look around. I think there's a crack in the roof."

She was right. Armed with pots and pans, we made our way into the living room. But after one look, we let them drop from our hands, horrified by what we saw.

Chapter 7

Two currents of water ran along the sloped ceiling, then joined in the corner to form a waterfall. The pans we had grabbed in the kitchen would fill too fast.

"I'll check the shed for something bigger," I shouted, heading for the door. We needed a five-gallon bucket, at least, and a backup for when the first one filled.

Two steps outside, the rain had soaked through my shirt. Talk about extreme weather. First an earthquake, then a monsoon. What next?

In the shed, Gram's love for gardening paid off. I found two buckets right away and raced back to the house. Paige passed me on the way.

"Where are you going?" I yelled over my shoulder.

"Gram sent me for a tarp and a ladder!"

Heebie Jeebies

I knew what that meant. I would have to climb on the roof to patch the crack. After setting up the buckets, I found Paige outside. She had a ladder but not a tarp.

"I couldn't find one," she said.

I searched the shed and garage but came up empty. On the verge of despair, Zack's name came to mind. When we had gone camping the previous summer, we used his tarp to cover the tent. Splashing my way back inside, I got on the phone and asked him to bring it over. Next, I helped Gram and Paige move furniture out of the way. Several more drips had formed at different points along the ceiling, turning our living room into a twelve-by-twelve shower, and a cold one at that.

Zack arrived a few minutes later with the blue nylon tarp. His brown hair was black from the rain. A drop of water shivered on the end of his nose like mercury.

"Thanks a lot, dude," I said, taking the tarp from him. He followed me through the living room to the back door.

"This is worse than I thought," he said, inspecting the damage.

"It was that earthquake," Gram said. She moved down the hall with a stack of magazines.

The Mysterious Treasure

Out back I leaned the ladder against the side of the house and headed up. Zack waited below with the tarp.

"As soon as you hand me the tarp, grab a hammer and nails from the shed." I pointed to the edge of the garden.

Zack looked all around, as if the shed was nowhere to be found.

"Zack? The shed's right there." I pointed again, while trying to keep my balance. Standing high on the ladder, I felt like a TV antenna, fully exposed to the sharp gusts and pelting rain.

"Nate, I know where the shed is," he shouted above the roar of the pounding rain. "That's not why I'm looking around. I thought I saw someone following me over here. It looked like Old Man Ingram."

"Why would Ingram follow you?" I asked.

"I don't know, but it's got me freaked out."

"Maybe he wants his spyglass back," I suggested, half-teasing.

"Maybe a *deal's a deal*," Zack countered, sounding defensive.

"Well, if Ingram does show up, we'll ask him to help. Now pay attention," I yelled.

Easing onto the roof, I crouched down low, not sure what to fear most: that the wood shingles would crumble beneath me like soggy crackers, or that the rain would make it a greased slide, and I'd slip off. Pushing my way higher, I lifted my foot from the top of the ladder until I was completely on the sloped shingles. So far so good. Zack followed with the tarp, climbing until he was just below the top of the ladder.

"Are you ready for this?" he asked, extending the tarp before I could answer.

"Not really, but I'll take it anyway," I said, taking the tarp. "Man, I knew Gram's roof was sloped more than most, but this is ridiculous."

With the rain running past me, it was like trying to sit still on a giant water slide. Inch by inch, I scaled higher on the roof, testing each shingle to make sure it would hold my weight. With the water and wind driving against me, the word *typhoon* came to mind.

When I reached the top, I sat with one leg on each side of the slope, finally feeling secure. Zack remained on the ladder, watching me and keeping an eye out for Ingram at the same time.

I knew the tarp wasn't big enough to cover the entire living room section of the roof, so I searched for the crack that was letting in the water.

"That might be it," I announced, thinking out loud. I scooted across the top several feet and felt

The Mysterious Treasure

a dark line in the shingles on the front side of the house. Sure enough, it was a crack like one would normally see in old concrete. It ran a jagged path from the top of the roof down.

"Found it!" I shouted.

Zack offered a thumbs up.

As quickly as possible, I spread the tarp across the long crack. Once it was in place, I edged to the back side of the roof and grabbed the hammer and nails from Zack. Ringlets that lined the edge of the tarp made it easy to tack it down without puncturing the waterproof fabric.

Just as I finished, Paige came running out the front door. "That's working, Nate! The water has practically stopped. You can come down."

"You don't have to ask twice," I muttered. "The sooner the better." The tarp was on the front side of the roof, opposite the ladder, so rather than climb back to the top of the shingles and down the other side, I decided to go down the side I was on.

With a quick glance below, I picked my route. A maple tree towered near the front corner of the house with plenty of branches. I had climbed on the roof from there once before, why not now? Edging my way over, I clung to the soaked shingles like a salamander.

"The key is friction," I whispered to myself.

Heebie Jeebies

"Nate, are you all right?" Zack shouted, unable to see me from the back.

"No problem," I answered, staying low. "I'm going down the front."

"What?" he called out.

I didn't bother to answer. I was too close to the tree. *I'll tell him when I get down.* One more foothold and I'd be there. *Easy, Nate.* I put my foot on a notch in the shingle. It held. *Now to reach for the branch.* I extended my arm. *A little farther.* I lifted myself from the roof and leaned out. *Almost there.* I went for it. Leaping out, I grabbed the branch. But instead of bark, I felt something slippery.

I gripped as tightly as I could, but it was no use. My hands slid down, as if clinging to a greased pole. I scraped past a lower branch and lost my grip entirely. I fell through the air as fast as the rain and hit the ground with a splat. As I struggled to regain my breath, I tried to figure out what bones I had broken. But everything seemed fine. In fact, the fall hadn't hurt as much as I thought it would. I sat for a moment in the mud and rain, then slowly rose to my feet. To steady myself, I reached for the trunk of the maple tree. As soon as I touched it, I drew my hand back in horror. I stared at my fingers, which were glowing with green slime.

Chapter 8

"Zack!" I yelled. "Come here! Quick!"

Pushing through the side gate, Zack found me beneath the maple tree, still gaping at my fingers.

"What happened?" he asked.

I explained my fall and what caused it. Zack slid some of the slime back and forth between his thumb and index finger.

"You probably just grabbed a slug," he said.

"A slug? I think I know what a slug is. This is the same stuff I found in the cave. And I don't even want to think about how it got here."

"Maybe the serpent is really a flying dragon," Zack suggested, tongue-in-cheek. "It probably flew over here when you weren't looking and perched in your maple tree to keep an eye on you."

"Listen to the comedian," I scoffed. "You're the one who's paranoid, not me. Quick, Zack, look! Old Man Ingram's hiding in the bushes, ready to jump out and get you."

"At least he really exists," Zack countered.

I was about to tell Zack to get lost, but I never got the chance. The electricity went out, dropping a sudden blackness on our house and street.

"Oh great," Zack exhaled, turning to survey the darkened neighborhood. "I'd better get home fast. If the power's out at our house, my mom will have a cow."

Without another word, he sprinted down the street, quickly disappearing in the gloomy rain. I headed through the front door, carefully feeling my way around the rearranged furniture and assortment of pots on the carpet. Soon Gram and Paige appeared from down the hall, holding lit candles. Paige extended one to me.

"Good work with the tarp," Gram said. "There's just a few slow leaks now. We should be fine until the storm passes. Then we'll see to getting the roof fixed."

"With what money?" I asked, feeling more pessimistic than usual.

"God will provide," Gram replied without hesitation. "He always does."

The Mysterious Treasure

"That's for sure," Paige added.

Normally I would have agreed, but tonight I didn't know what to say. I stared at my candle as a drop of water landed next to the wick, almost putting it out.

After two hours of sopping up carpet puddles with every towel in the house, I was exhausted and ready to climb into bed. The power was still out, but my candle burned brightly.

From the living room, I could hear water drops falling into the pans, each releasing a unique tone, like different sized bells. At first it sounded cool, but then it began to grate on me. I covered my head with my pillow, but I could still hear the hollow plink, plank, plunk each time a drop landed in the stainless steel.

Gradually, my attitude turned worse and worse. *Why am I even living in this little house?* I lamented. If my parents hadn't drowned years ago, Paige and I would be living with them in a big, dry house with an ocean view. Dad was an architect before he died. Our house certainly wouldn't leak. Not that I blamed Gram. She did what she could with what little money she earned at the garden store. Combined with Grandad's insurance, we got by. Every last dime was accounted for . . . and pinched.

Heebie Jeebies

As the rain splattered over the tarp, the wind turned into a giant whip, snapping the house from the north. Lying awake, I thought more and more about my mom and dad. I wondered whether they thought about me and Paige when their boat was going down. I wondered what they would have told us about God and life and the sea. I knew that a sudden and terrible storm had capsized their boat, but not much else. Gram avoided talking about it, and I never knew whether she was avoiding the subject for our benefit or hers.

I hated nights like this. The night my parents died, I slept through the storm as sound as ever, like I didn't have a care in the world. Now I stared at the ceiling, awake and lonely, longing for a mom and dad to fix leaky roofs and pay for repairs and chase off serpents in the night.

Before my attitude could drop any further, I decided to read from the Bible. At the beginning of the year I had decided to read through the entire Bible, one chapter a night. I knew it'd take about three years to completely finish, but I didn't care. I just wanted to read through from start to finish. Since January, I had read almost every night. And the few nights I missed, I made up the following evening. To stay on my schedule, I needed to get

The Mysterious Treasure

through the twenty-seventh chapter of Isaiah tonight before falling asleep.

Normally I would read several verses at a time, then pause to think about what I'd learned. But tonight, halfway through the first verse, my mouth dropped open.

"In that day," I read, "the Lord will punish with his sword, his fierce, great and powerful sword, Leviathan the gliding serpent, Leviathan the coiling serpent; he will slay the monster of the sea."

My pounding heart jolted me straight up in bed.

"That's it," I gasped.

"What's that?" Gram called down the hall.

"Sorry, Gram," I responded. "I'm just thinking out loud." I tried to sit still and be quiet, but that wasn't easy. Every bone in my body was trembling. The sea cave monster was no longer a mystery. It was Leviathan. It had to be. The verse described it as a gliding serpent. How could it glide unless it was covered with slime?

I turned to the back of my Bible to find other references on Leviathans. The word came up again in Job 41. Turning there, I read verses 8 and 9 and my bones felt like they would melt away. "If you lay a hand on him, you will remember the struggle and never do it again! Any hope of subduing him is false; the mere sight of him is overpowering."

Heebie Jeebies

That's for sure, I thought. The tail that slithered away from me in the cave looked like the tail of a dinosaur. It was overpowering, and then some. The more I thought about it, the more amazed I was that we had made it out of the sea cave alive. Maybe God would one day crush the Leviathan, but I sure wasn't up for the job.

As the wax disappeared beneath the hungry flame, I kept my eye on the window. The rain had a temper now, lashing at the glass in torrents. Along with the angry water came branches and leaves, just outside the glass, snapping in the wind like a dragon's tail. At least, it looked like branches and leaves. Maybe it was something else. With the description of Leviathan so fresh in my mind, I couldn't stop thinking about it.

My practical side said not to worry. The Bible described it as a sea monster. Even if it was in the sea cave, how would it get up here? The raging outside continued. Then a crunching sound approached the window, just a few feet away. I had to look.

The candle's heat warmed my temple as I approached the window. I considered going to retrieve my dive flashlight to pierce the darkness, but there was no time for that. I leaned forward until the tip of my nose touched the cool pane. The

The Mysterious Treasure

flame danced in the window to the rhythm of the wind. Being so close to the outdoors gave me the heebie jeebies. Leviathan could crash through the glass and swallow my head in one swift motion.

Crunch! Twigs snapped just outside my window.

I dropped the candle on the carpet. Hot wax splashed over my bare feet as the flame was snuffed out. I hopped around in pain but couldn't shout out. Gram would come in and want an explanation. Steadying myself, I peered into the stormy night. I remembered Mom and Dad and wondered whether their mystery had been solved. Had a Leviathan charged their boat like a torpedo? Had it come back for me and Paige?

Crunch!

Something was definitely out there. But what? I searched intently.

A long, shiny image glided into a clump of bushes a few feet from my window. Was that the Leviathan? It held still. But maybe that was its plan. It would leave the midsection of its body stationary, while the jaws and endless rows of teeth eased into position beneath my window. I leaned back, just in case. In the darkness, the creature's details were lost. The skin appeared greenish-brown, and seemed to rise and fall with each breath. I couldn't be sure.

But I wouldn't give up either. If necessary, I'd wait up all night, staring out the window at the serpent in the leaves.

Chapter 9

I don't know when I fell asleep or when the power came back on. When I awoke, my red neon alarm clock was flashing 12:00. Jumping to the window, the first thing I did was search for the Leviathan. In the spot where I thought I had seen the serpent, a stone about two feet long and a foot high rested in the soft mud. Damp leaves covered most of the surface, giving it a shiny, snake-like appearance.

Ok, so maybe what I saw wasn't the Leviathan, but that didn't mean that my impression of something out there was ridiculous. On the ground alongside the house, a trail of leaves had been matted into the ground. Something was out there, I decided. With so much rain, I couldn't tell whether the branches were covered with green slime or water.

Not a problem. It would just take a few minutes to find out.

As I was getting dressed, the phone rang. It was Zack, all pumped up to explore the sea cave.

"Let's check it out," Zack urged.

"In this weather?" I asked. "The waves will be huge. And thanks to the run-off from the storm, the visibility will be terrible. What's the point?"

"Treasure!" Zack cheered. "That's the point."

"Whatever treasure is in that cave, will be there when the visibility improves. Let's just wait a few days." Reading the Bible verses about the Leviathan reduced my cave exploration desire to zilch. But after what Zack said last night, I knew there was no point in telling him anything.

"How about this?" Zack suggested. "We'll use the sea kayak. It's unsinkable. Not only that, we'll be at the sea cave in a flash. If we get there and the water's too rough, we'll just check things out and call it a day."

I could tell Zack wouldn't take no for an answer. I reluctantly agreed to go along because I knew that otherwise he would go alone. And if something went wrong, there'd be no one to help him.

While gathering up my skin-diving gear, I mulled over how to convince Gram to let me go. I

The Mysterious Treasure

checked her room and the kitchen but couldn't find her. Heading into the living room, I found Paige on the couch watching TV.

"Where's Gram?" I asked.

"She had some errands to run," Paige said. "I asked her if I could go with her, but she was pretty secretive about the whole thing."

"Well, when she comes back, tell her I went kayaking with Zack."

"To the sea cave?" Paige asked.

Paige's interest made me nervous. "I doubt we'll go *in* the sea cave. But Zack wants to at least look at it."

"That's not fair," Paige complained, turning off the TV. "I'm the one who helped you find it."

I shrugged. "Sorry. The sea kayak only holds two people."

Paige crossed her arms, sulking in the couch. "When Gram comes home, I'll make *sure* she knows where you are."

"Great," I muttered, heading out the door. First Zack talks me into a trip on a storm-tossed sea, then my sister pledges to get me in trouble for it.

Outside, the wind and rain had subsided, but clouds still covered Starboard like rag wool.

Zack was waiting at his house with all of his gear stored in the sea kayak's watertight compartments. I stowed my gear too, and we headed for the beach.

Zack's dad had built a small cart to make it easy to wheel the fully loaded kayak to the bay.

Once we reached the water's edge, I took a deep breath. I always forgot how cold the ocean felt in the morning. Fortunately, it was only around my legs. Climbing to the front of the kayak, I paddled hard as Zack shoved off from the beach. As soon as he was seated, we dug into the water with arms straining, determined to beat the waves. Normally, the bay has little, if any, surf; but with the storm, whitecaps tossed in every direction.

"Outside," I yelled, spotting a massive wave on the horizon.

We paddled hard for the deep water along the cliffs that shielded the sea cave. Waves seldom broke there until they hit the rocks. As long as we stayed offshore, we'd be fine.

"Harder," Zack shouted.

We drove at the sea with all our might but didn't make it. The wave broke in front of us like a waterfall, turning our shirts into sponges. Amazingly, we didn't tip over. The white water boiled under us like frothed milk and knocked us back to the beach. Tired and wet, we had to start over. We didn't get far

The Mysterious Treasure

before another wave hit us, and another. We struggled ahead, our muscles burning at first, then cramping.

"What'd I tell you about the storm, Zack?" I reminded him.

"Don't give up on me now, Nate," he shouted over the roar of tumbling surf. "Just think treasure."

"Sure," I replied. "Give me treasure or give me death."

"Now you're talking."

"I was kidding," I grunted, digging deep with the paddle. Another wave crashed in front of us, spraying our faces with silver flakes. Soaked and salty, we continued.

Our determination didn't come without a reward. When we passed over the top of a giant wave before it broke, we knew that we had made it. The water was still rough and layered with whitecaps, but nothing like the pounding waves we had just endured.

"This we can handle," Zack said.

Easing up, we let our arms recuperate.

"Just keep us on course for the sea cave," Zack reminded me.

"Don't worry," I said.

Once we reached the cliffs at the north end of the bay, I knew it was only a couple hundred more yards. The only trick now was dodging rocks just below the surface. Even though it was low tide, the water level wasn't as low as when Paige and I made the trip. Bride Rock was one of the few rocks that still broke the surface. It towered over us a like a monument.

"What are you doing?" Zack asked the minute I quit paddling.

"Feeling for rocks," I told him. I pushed my paddle into the water in front of us.

"I don't see anything," he said.

"Neither do I. That's the problem. This water's like mud." I was about to lift my paddle when it bumped something. "There you are," I said, addressing the rock. I turned the kayak toward deeper water. After heading north about fifty feet, I brought it back in, convinced we were past a triangle of rocks that, in lower seas, would have protruded into the air.

Pushing north again, with the salt and spray lashing at our faces, we arrived at the section of cliff that housed the sea cave. I would have pointed it out to Zack, but the big surf hid the mouth entirely. Beneath us, the sea heaved and dropped, like a giant blue blanket snapping in the wind.

"You're sure it's there?" Zack questioned.

"Positive."

The Mysterious Treasure

"Then let's have a closer look," Zack said, paddling for the sea cave's location.

"You're nuts," I countered. "I'd rather kayak through a tornado than one of those waves."

"They're not that—"

Before Zack could say another word, a swell rolled beneath us. We buoyed up, then dropped back down. At the cliff, the wave's bottom dropped out as the peak rose, creating a ten-foot face that slammed against the rocks with locomotive force.

"On second thought," Zack added, sounding slightly more intimidated. "I've got a better idea." I could hear him reaching into one of the sealed bins and rustling through his gear. When I turned around, one eye was shut and the other was pressed against the end of his spyglass.

"That was the best twenty bucks you ever spent," I said, waiting for a report.

"I saw it! The sea cave. It was just the top, but when the tide receded after a wave, I saw the opening."

"I told you, didn't I?" Turning around, I hoped to catch a glimpse of the hole that had created such a haunting impression on my life in the last twenty-four hours.

"I don't believe it!" Zack announced.

I immediately thought of the Leviathan. "What'd you see?"

Heebie Jeebies

"Someone is with Ingram, in his house."

"What?" I turned to see Zack with the spyglass directed high above the sea cave. "Who is it?"

"Can't tell. Ingram moved over and blocked my view."

"Let me see that thing." I extended my hand, waiting for my turn with the spyglass. For years no one had entered Ingram's mansion. That wasn't idle speculation; that was fact. Everyone in town attested to it, including his neighbors.

Once Zack turned over the spyglass, I adjusted the focus then searched the windows for Ingram. I found him on the first floor, with his back to the sea. At first I couldn't see anyone with him. But then he moved and another person's arm and shoulder came into view. I couldn't tell if it was a man or woman. Before I could find out, he or she retreated. Ingram responded by raising his fist and turning toward the window. His face was red, and wet. He beat the glass and screamed at the sea. The person behind him stepped forward.

"Just a little closer," I said, hoping to get a look at the person's face. "That's it. Almost." I adjusted the lens to sharpen the focus.

Then the spyglass went black. "No!"

"What do you mean, *no?*" Zack asked.

"Your cheap spyglass broke. I can't see a thing."

The Mysterious Treasure

"Let me see that."

I handed it over. Zack checked the lens and adjusted the focus but to no avail.

"What'd you do to it?" he demanded.

"Nothing," I said, defensively.

"Then why won't it work?" Zack shook it like a can of Parmesan cheese. "If I have to take this in, you're paying for the repair."

"Forget you. I just tried to adjust the focus." I turned back to Ingram's mansion, but the window was empty. It wouldn't have mattered anyway. Without the spyglass, it would be impossible to make out a face. "Great. Now they're both gone."

"Who cares about Ingram?" Zack grumbled. "My spyglass is ruined."

"In that case, use it for a paddle. We're drifting toward the cliffs."

"I'll use you for a paddle in a minute."

I was about to come up with a challenge of my own, when I realized how bad I would feel if something I cherished got ruined.

"Hey, I'm sorry about the spyglass. I'll pay for the repair."

Zack didn't trust my sudden change of heart. "With what money?"

I shrugged. "I don't know. But I know God will provide somehow. He always does."

Heebie Jeebies

"Not that God stuff again," Zack objected.

"What do you mean by that? If the Lord wasn't looking out for us, we'd both be long gone by now. Especially after all the psycho stuff we've been through, like shark dives without cages and cliff climbing without ropes and *this*."

Normally, Zack was ready with a snappy comeback. But he held his tongue, like I was finally getting through to him. I decided to push ahead and see if he was ready to talk about his beliefs and maybe even make a commitment to Christ. From previous efforts, I knew he understood the basics of the gospel.

But before I could say another word, something bumped the bottom of the boat.

"Woah!" Zack hollered.

"What was that?" I asked, quickly grabbing my paddle.

"Probably just a fish," Zack suggested. He quickly returned the spyglass to the zippered pouch and grabbed his paddle.

"Since when do fish attack kayaks?" I asked.

"Since one of the crew is paranoid of—"

Zack didn't finish. He couldn't.

With the force of a rising submarine, something rose from the depths and flipped our kayak like a coin. Gasping for air, we clung to the capsized boat.

The Mysterious Treasure

I expected a thousand tiny teeth to latch onto my ankles and pull me down.

"Paranoid, huh?" I scoffed.

"It could have been a rock," he offered.

"Sure. A rock comes to life on a mission to destroy."

When a quick thrust of water pulled around my ankles, I stared at Zack. He knew what I was thinking and admitted to feeling the same thing.

We stared at the lead-colored water, fearing the worst. Then beside me I saw the hump of something long and green. "Did you see that?" I asked.

"See what?"

"It rose beside me."

"Are you sure it wasn't a wake?"

"You're still doubting?" I fumed.

"Sorry, but I don't know what to believe."

"Then maybe this will help," I said. I put Zack's hand on the side panel of the overturned kayak. Rather than jerk away, he just left it there, as if stuck permanently with slime.

Chapter 10

The next few days weighed like gray ice on our shoulders. The clouds over Starboard were screwed down tight as a lid, but it never rained. A red tide spread through the sea, mixing with the already brown run-off. Water visibility was reduced to zero. The heavy surf continued to pound the shore. Needless to say, skin diving was off limits.

Zack and I didn't talk much after our trip to the sea cave. Getting the kayak to shore that day was a nightmare. We used what little strength we had left to right the thing and climb back in. On the way back, the wind turned against us. With the crashing surf and spray blasting our faces, it felt like we were paddling through a car wash.

The spyglass was also a problem. Zack still blamed me for its failure.

But the hardest thing to deal with, by far, was Gram's moodiness. She shifted from despair to delight, and back again several times a day. She scared me and Paige too. We wondered whether the weight of poverty, and a deteriorating house that she couldn't afford to fix, had finally gotten the best of her. She became increasingly mysterious. We feared that she had lost her mind completely. If she was on the phone, she'd lower her voice when we walked by, or she'd make calls from her bedroom with the door closed.

"Maybe she's talking to creditors," I told Paige one afternoon when Gram was gone. Minutes later the phone rang. I picked up the receiver, hoping to find out. But no such luck. It was Zack.

"Nate, take a hammer to your piggy bank," Zack said. "I found a guy who fixes spyglasses."

"You're serious?"

"No and yes. I don't need your money, but I really did find a spyglass repair shop."

"Sounds good," I said. "I'll be right over."

Paige wanted to come along, but, with Gram out, I knew she should keep an eye on the house. Zack's tarp was still on the roof, but it didn't stop all the drips. If it started to rain, she could move pots to the needed areas.

The Mysterious Treasure

I found Zack in his front yard; and we headed downtown, past the bank and post office to a street lined with some of Starboard's older buildings.

"That's it," Zack said, directing my attention across the street.

"But that's Moby's," I objected.

The building Zack pointed to was one of the first erected in Starboard. The gray siding looked like it was salvaged from an old whaling ship. For all we knew, it was. The first floor housed one of the most popular cafes in town. It featured fresh seafood and patio dining. Because of its location, locals gathered like sea gulls. Beneath the thatched umbrellas made of dried palm leaves, they'd talk with friends as they passed by.

"Pequod's Periscopes is on the second floor," Zack said.

Until now I had never given much thought to what was on the second floor. A quick glance at the outdoor staircase made me wish it could stay that way. The stairs leading up were made of the same weathered wood as the rest of the building. It seemed they would collapse beneath the first person who tried to climb them. And where they led didn't look too keen either. There was hardly a window on the second floor, making it appear as dreary as it was decrepit. A tree that grew along the stairs had branches that spread like a vulture's wings over the doors. It looked like some kind of dark tower, where a king would banish an enemy.

"Are you sure we can't fix the spyglass ourselves?" I suggested, not wanting to brave those stairs.

"We've been through this already. Even if I could open this thing up, I wouldn't want to risk moving the lenses. If they get out of position, the spyglass will never work right. Now come on." Zack stepped into the street, then stopped suddenly and grabbed my arm.

I figured that a truck was barreling down, ready to mow us over. But the street was empty.

"What's wrong?" I asked.

Zack didn't answer. He just backed me to the bus stop and motioned for me to get down.

Crouched behind the bench, I asked again. "What's wrong?"

"It's Old Man Ingram," Zack whispered. "He's at one of the tables."

"You're nuts. He never leaves his house."

"Look!"

Sure enough, Old Man Ingram sat alone under one of the thatched umbrellas. His face was weathered. His hair weighed on his head like the clouds over Starboard. A manila envelope served as a

The Mysterious Treasure

place mat in front of him, held in place by a cup of coffee.

"What's the big deal?" I asked. "If Ingram's having garage sales and people to his house, so what if he goes out to eat?"

"It's not the eating that bothers me. It's that everywhere I go, he goes."

"Not that again."

"Yes, that! I saw him watching me the other day when I walked by his house. Then I saw him again at Joe's Wharf. I turned around, and he was tracking me."

I squinted hard, thinking. "It is kind of weird that the one time we come to Pequod's Periscopes he's at the same building . . . waiting."

"Tell me about it. There's no way I'm walking right past him. He'll probably ask for the spyglass back."

"Either that or follow us upstairs to that dark tower," I added.

Zack wouldn't give up. "Let's see if there's a staircase around back."

We backtracked to a point where we could cross the street without being seen. Then we walked through the alley behind the row of stores. But when we got to Moby's no alternate stairs could be found. Rather than return to the bus stop, we decided to edge along the side of the restaurant, hoping to make a quick spin up the stairs without being seen.

"Almost there," Zack said.

We clung to the wood like spiders. At the front corner, we chanced a quick look, hoping Ingram would be gone or have his face buried in his menu. We froze in our tracks and stared in awe at what we saw . . .

Chapter 11

Sitting across from Ingram, Gram was staring at her hands, as if too afraid to look him in the face.

Mr. Ingram lifted his coffee cup and quickly slid the manila envelope across the table to Gram. As he did, he spoke to her, but we couldn't hear what he said.

Gram just stared at the envelope, unwilling to touch it, like she wasn't ready to accept its contents. Then tears fell from her eyes, and she quickly used her napkin to hide her face.

"What's going on?" I stammered under my breath.

"It can't be good," Zack decided.

"It probably has to do with our house," I guessed. "Old Man Ingram owns half the town. He's probably foreclosing on us."

Heebie Jeebies

"No way. Your Gram has lived there too long. The mortgage must be paid off by now. Then again, her face just keeps getting wetter."

I held my breath in hopes of hearing at least a fragment of their conversation. But the clang of dishes and other diners conversing squelched Gram's voice. "This stinks," I said, looking for a closer place to watch. But before I could take another step, Gram rose from the table and turned to leave. As an afterthought, she grabbed the envelope.

"I've got to know what's going on," I said. When Zack grabbed my arm, I twisted free and marched for the tables. Stomping past Mr. Ingram, I trailed Gram and finally caught her two stores down.

"Where did you come from?" Gram asked. She moved the envelope behind her back, as if it didn't exist.

I ignored her question. "Are you all right? What did Old Man Ingram say to you? And what's in there?"

Her lips tightened. "That's none of your business. Since when do you have the right to spy on me? I think *you're* the one who owes *me* an explanation."

I quickly backpeddled. "I was only trying to help."

The Mysterious Treasure

"You can help by allowing me some privacy. Now, do you have somewhere to go, or do you want to wait around for me to ground you?"

Dumbfounded, I did an about-face and returned to Moby's. Gram's cold reproach made me even more angry with Mr. Ingram. Even though I couldn't tell him off, I'd give him a look that accomplished the same thing. But by the time I returned to the patio, he was gone.

Zack was at the top of the stairs waiting for me.

"Well?" he asked.

"Gram shot me down like a rusty pelican. What happened to Old Man Ingram?"

"As soon as you and your Gram left, he got up and walked away."

"Which way did he go?" I demanded.

"How should I know? I ducked down so he wouldn't see me."

I rubbed my eyes in frustration; this was yet another mysterious twist in a week of bizarre events.

Zack grabbed the doorknob to Pequod's, determined to move ahead. When the door wouldn't open, we rang the bell.

Footsteps clopped across the floor as someone approached from the other side.

Heebie Jeebies

"Sounds like cement shoes to me," I said.

Before Zack could respond, the door squeaked open. A man with wire-rim glasses, fuzzy ears, and black boots stood before us. "One of you must be Zack," he said, inviting us in.

"Right here," Zack replied. He held up the spyglass for Pequod to inspect.

"This is a beauty, isn't it?" Pequod said. "A 1931 Zwiess, if I'm not mistaken. Good thing you came by. It's definitely worth fixing."

Pequod's shop was full of scopes of various lengths. A telescope rested on a brass tripod next to the front window. Binoculars hung from a rusty fishhook large enough to catch a whale.

"Looks like we found the right place," I said.

Pequod didn't answer. His attention was on the spyglass. He held it to his eye and adjusted the focus. "There's something blocking your lenses, all right. You boys have a seat. Give me a few minutes, and we'll find out what's wrong."

Zack and I watched Pequod place the spyglass on his workbench. He took out some specialty tools that I had never seen before. With surprising speed, he removed the outer casing. He didn't have to explain what caused the trouble. We could see it for ourselves. Wedged between the front and back lenses was a folded piece of paper.

The Mysterious Treasure

Pequod carefully lifted the paper from the spyglass and handed it to Zack. "Now that's something. It's hard to imagine how that got in there."

Zack unfolded the piece of faded paper. It was crisp and thin, like the paper you'd find in an expensive Bible. Even before he opened it all the way, we could tell it had something on it. I figured it was a diagram for the spyglass, until I saw the drawing.

For the longest time we didn't say a word. The shock was too much. When Zack finally spoke, it was in fragments.

"Trea . . . sure," he muttered. "Th-this is a treasure m-map."

When Pequod snatched up the map, I thought Zack would go for his throat.

"It's definitely a map," Pequod agreed. "And this poem obviously implies some kind of treasure."

We gathered around and read the words:

When the tide is out go in
When the tide is in you win
The anchor is your treasure.

Zack pulled the map from Pequod and held it like a thousand-dollar bill. "This oblong section must be a pond. These waving lines must be a stream that flows from it. The stream then leads to the ocean."

"That's the longest pond I've ever seen," Pequod said.

"Since when can't ponds be long?" Zack asked, getting bothered.

As Pequod and Zack argued back and forth, I stared at the map until a light flicked on in my head. Of course. Pequod was right. That was no pond, or stream, for that matter. But it was definitely a treasure map. And I knew the exact location. But I wasn't about to say anything to Zack until no one else could hear.

"Well, I guess we'll just have to find out," I said, interrupting them both. "Now how much do I owe you?"

"Leave the map, and it's on me," Pequod said.

"No chance," Zack answered.

Pequod grumbled at us both while putting the outer casing back on the spyglass. "Ten bucks, then."

Putting the money on the workbench, I quickly ushered Zack to the alley.

"Well?" Zack asked, knowing I had something to say.

"You won't believe it."

"Try me."

The Mysterious Treasure

"This is the sea cave. You were right about the ocean. But this isn't a pond and a stream. It's a cavern and a tunnel leading to it. It's the sea cave under Old Man Ingram's mansion. Pirates must have discovered it years ago."

"That's it! They buried a treasure there, then filled in the cave. It stayed that way until last week's earthquake." Zack let out a laugh. "Ingram would be sick if he knew about this. He not only let me have an antique spyglass for twenty bucks. Without knowing it, he threw in a treasure map too."

I wasn't so quick to join in Zack's laughter. "What if he somehow clued in *after* he sold you the spyglass? Maybe that's why he's been watching you. He's waiting for a chance to get it back."

"Too bad if he is," Zack snapped. "A deal's a deal."

For the next few minutes, neither of us said a word. We just stared at the map, with its detailed marks and figures, dreaming of treasure.

Chapter 12

Before discovering the treasure map, Zack's desire to see the sea cave was high enough. Now it bordered on dangerous.

"It's got to be tomorrow morning," he said, pacing back and forth in my room, unable to contain himself. "We'll have low tide and calm winds."

"What about the swell and poor visibility?" I asked.

"We'll have to make do. Besides, it's only going to get worse. A big swell is supposed to hit by tomorrow night."

The map was on the desk in front of me. I looked it over for the hundredth time, wondering what kind of treasure lay buried beneath the sand at the end of the cavern. An "X" on the map seemed to indicate we'd find the treasure there. I imagined an old wooden chest with brass hinges, loaded to the brim with gold coins and jewels.

We had spent the afternoon planning and loading our gear in the kayak. Along with our usual assortment of skin-diving equipment, we included shovels and a lantern. We also made repeated trips to the bay to check on conditions.

As much as I hated to admit it, Zack's timing made sense. The longer we waited, the better chance someone else had of discovering the cave. And given the condition of our leaky roof, if in fact it still was *our* roof, we could certainly use the money.

There was just one problem—one big slimy problem: the Leviathan.

Knock! Knock!

"Who's that?" Zack gasped, as if we were plotting to overthrow the government.

I shrugged and walked to the door. "Yeah?"

"It's me," Paige said. "Let me in."

I closed the door behind her and waited for an update. She just shook her head. "Gram wouldn't say a thing."

I moaned. "Did you come right out and ask her?"

"No," Paige said, getting defensive. "What am I supposed to say, 'Nate saw you crying when Old

THE MYSTERIOUS TREASURE

Man Ingram gave you an envelope? What's in it? Huh? Fess up, Gram. We really want to know.'"

"Don't get smart with me," I told her. "You're a girl. You're supposed to know how to get information out of people. Think of Delilah with Samson. She was a pro. She wouldn't take no for an answer."

"Well, I'm not Delilah. And you're the one who saw the envelope; maybe you should ask Gram yourself."

"I already tried that. She wouldn't tell me anything."

"So try again. Don't take no for an answer." Paige offered a smirk, as if to say, "Gotcha."

I looked at Zack for support, but he was so engrossed in the map, he didn't hear a word we said.

"Where's Gram?" I asked.

"In her room, I think," Paige replied. "See you in a bit." She moved to the desk to study the map with Zack.

Cracking open my door, I stepped lightly down the hall. Gram's bedroom door was closed. Before knocking, I mulled over what to say. The indirect approach seemed the best. I hoped that if I hinted around enough, Gram would bring up the envelope on her own.

Heebie Jeebies

Squeezing my knuckles together, I lifted my hand. But that's as far as I got. Gram's broken voice came from inside.

"It's just not fair," she sobbed. "Why do these things have to happen? Why?"

I stared at the door, feeling a hatred in my heart for Old Man Ingram. It had to be him. First he hovers over the ocean like a black vulture. Then he forecloses on our home. What else could have been in that envelope? In the ten years we had lived with Gram, I had never seen her cry. Now she couldn't stop.

Turning around, I tiptoed back to my room and closed the door.

"Well?" Paige asked. "Did you talk to her?"

"Not this time," I said, determined to protect Paige from what I had heard. "Maybe I'll try again later."

Returning my attention to the sea cave, I suggested that we make one last scouting trip to the cliffs to check the condition of the surf. Zack was quick to agree and grabbed his spyglass and map. Paige asked to come along, and I didn't hesitate to say yes. I wanted her out of the house so Gram could have time to herself.

After ushering Zack and Paige to the kitchen, I left Gram a short note. I explained that the three of

The Mysterious Treasure

us had gone on a walk to the ocean and would be back soon.

We stepped outside into the damp night air. A frigid evening wind had kicked up. Thick gray clouds still hovered over Starboard. I longed for a full moon and a host of stars, or anything else that would lift the dreary umbrella from our town.

Paige must have felt the same way because she grabbed my arm and matched me stride for stride, determined to stay close.

When Zack headed for the pier in the center of the beach that bordered Starboard, I objected.

"We should scope out the ocean as close to the cliffs as possible, since that's where we'll be skin diving," I tried to convince him.

"How close?" Zack asked.

I knew what he was thinking. The farther north we moved along the cliffs, the closer we would be to Mr. Ingram's. But I didn't care. I wanted to see how the surf looked at the sea cave. If the waves were crashing as heavy as I feared, the morning dive might not be possible. And there was another reason: the Leviathan. I needed to look down on the water and *not* see it, before getting psyched up to return.

Walking along Ridgeview Street, it was hard not to marvel at the estates that lined the cliff. Broad manicured lawns spread from the curb to the mansions. Floodlights bought to life the flowers that accented the landscaping. Just looking at the order and calm made it hard to imagine the chaos behind them, a sea in turmoil, rolling like thunder below their back yards.

"So tell me, Nate," Zack asked. "Where do you expect to find a sea view on this street?"

I kept walking. "In the vacant lot up ahead. And don't worry, it's still a ways from Old Man Ingram's."

Zack shook his head. "Guess again. A developer put a fence across that vacant lot."

"So we'll hop the fence."

"Sure. You tie up the guard dog, then we'll join you."

"I guess we'll just have to find the next open lot," I said. We all knew what that meant. The Ingram estate covered three lots. The house sat on the center one. The lots on each side remained in their natural state. The unaltered shrubs and wild flowers looked the same to us as they would have to a pirate two hundred years ago.

When we arrived at the edge of the property, Zack crossed his arms. "For some reason I knew we were destined to end up here."

"Believe me," I said, remembering the envelope that had made Gram cry. "It's not my first choice

The Mysterious Treasure

either. But we might as well get used to it. Tonight we're beside his place. Tomorrow we'll be under it."

Zack stared at the mansion as though it were haunted. I didn't blame him. With its smoky windows and splintered siding, it was hard to imagine it as anything else.

"Are we going to check out the surf or not?" Paige asked, getting impatient.

Zack pointed at the thick growth that rose between us and the cliff's edge. "You first."

Pushing my way through the bushes, I quickly forgot about Old Man Ingram. My thoughts were 100 percent Leviathan. With each branch I grabbed, I expected the green slime to squeeze through my fingers.

Then Paige said something, and I turned around. Bad timing. My right foot came down and kept going. There was no ground to stop it. I had reached the edge of the cliff.

"Ahhh!" I screamed out, backpeddling in the air.

Paige grabbed my arm and pulled, while Zack slapped a hand over my mouth.

"What are you, crazy?" they both snapped in unison.

"You try leading in the dark," I countered.

Zack searched through the bushes toward the mansion. "Old Man Ingram probably heard you."

Heebie Jeebies

"So what if he did?" I replied. "He may be cruel, but at least we know what we're dealing with."

"So that's it?" Zack scowled. "You're freaked out over that Leviathan thing again."

"Look who's talking," I shot back. "You're so freaked over the old man, you're afraid to even be near his house."

Zack shrugged and looked around, unwilling to admit I was right.

Standing at the edge of the cliff, we studied the water below. It was the color of lead, broken by splashes of white foam. The waves had died down but were still attacking the cliff. The old sea lion rested atop Bride Rock, bellowing now and then. Otherwise, all we could hear was the wind drawing past our ankles into the brush.

"There it is," I said, pointing.

To get a better view, Zack bumped past Paige, practically launching her over the cliff.

"Watch it!" Paige said.

Zack ignored her. "Where is it? I don't see it."

"Don't worry, it's there," I said.

"Then are you satisfied?" Zack asked. "Are you ready for a morning dive?"

"Not really," I lamented. "But with tomorrow's low tide, I hope we'll be ok."

The Mysterious Treasure

"We'll be better than that," Zack added. "We'll be rich."

"Says who?" an unnaturally deep voice called out.

Zack, Paige, and I exchanged glances. We couldn't see the person speaking but had a pretty good idea who it was: Old Man Ingram.

We scrambled through the bushes like weasels, determined to find freedom in the street. Zack and I pushed ahead, reaching it before Paige.

"Help me," she shouted.

I did an about-face and moved to the rescue. When I saw Paige's hand rising from the ground, I grabbed hold to pull her up. Running for the street, we bumped into Zack. He had his spyglass stuck to his eye, staring up at the mansion.

"Come on," I said, directing him on.

As the three of us ran down the street, I asked Zack what he saw.

"It was Old Man Ingram in the window, with a spyglass against his eye, staring back at me."

"Then whose voice did we hear coming from the lot?"

"I don't know," Zack replied. "I really don't know."

Chapter 13

The next morning, all three of us pulled the kayak down to the water. As we did, a sense of dread and anticipation came over me, and I realized that the moment of truth had finally come.

"You got the map?" I asked Zack.

Zack exhaled with disgust. "Of course I've got it."

I should have seen that coming. After the way he acted last night, he probably slept with it under his pillow.

The voice from last night was still a mystery. After leaving the cliff, we had gone with Zack to his house, which kept us out a little longer. By the time we got home, Gram had left for a walk. When she returned, we were already in bed. I tried to fall asleep but couldn't; and so for the longest time I listened to Gram move throughout the house, praying that she would stay away from the envelope, or phone, or anything else that would make her cry.

Before climbing in the kayak, Zack gathered us in a circle and put his hands in the center. He waited for us to do the same. "Give me treasure, or give me death!" he chanted. "Come on. Let's hear it!"

Paige and I exchanged glances, then took up the pledge with Zack. I hoped he was kidding, but it was hard to tell.

After getting situated in the kayak, we paddled for the sea cave. I sat in front. Zack played captain in the stern position. Paige clung to the end of the boat, dangling her legs in the water. The plan was for her to be our human outboard motor, but from what I could tell, she just coasted.

"You make good shark bait," Zack told her.

"Thanks a bunch," she said dryly.

A thick layer of fog covered the water, but at least the swell had died down. Instead of mountainous waves and sharp whitecaps, the ocean looked more like a plowed field. Traveling was a breeze, and in just minutes we arrived at the sea cave.

First we anchored the kayak, then we put on our masks, fins, and snorkels, along with neoprene booties to protect our feet inside the cave. Before taking the extra gear in with us, we decided to

The Mysterious Treasure

show Zack the way and make sure everything was the way we remembered it.

"I'll go first," I said. Surprisingly, Zack didn't object. I led the way to the mouth of the sea cave. With the low tide, the top half was exposed and remained above water at least ten feet back. It still looked like a whale's mouth but even hungrier than before, like it hadn't eaten in days.

Looking down its jagged throat, I paused to say a prayer.

"Ready?" I asked Zack and Paige.

They nodded.

Breathing heavily through our snorkels, we kicked to the back of the cave where the ceiling met the surface of the water. There we took several deep breaths and dove like submarines. The visibility was terrible. I wondered if we were in a sea cave or a clogged drain. Thousand of particles swirled in front of my dive light.

I kicked as hard as I could, tracing my light along the ceiling. I didn't know what to fear more, the Leviathan or drowning. I swam harder, my heart pounding. I needed air, and soon! Paige and Zack were right behind me. I couldn't turn around. With the incoming waves, I might not even make it back out.

Keep going, I told myself. Push!

Finally, the rocks lifted away from the surface of the water. It was open. I thrust my head into the open air and gulped down breath after breath. Damp, salty air never tasted so good. Soon Zack and Paige rose next to me and did the same.

The cavern looked just as I remembered it. The ceiling rose like a tower above us, high into the cliff. The walls were smooth, except for dozens of thin cracks, lined with crabs. Climbing would be impossible. Clumps of matted seaweed covered the rocks at our feet like old fishing nets.

"So far so good," I said, climbing out of the water onto the small beach at the end of cavern.

Paige cleared her throat. "Nate, I think you spoke too soon." Her light was focused on a rock next to her foot. Beneath the beam, shiny and wet, was a pile of green slime.

"We're toast," I conceded, joining my light with hers. I searched around, and found more green slime just beneath the surface of the water. It was everywhere. The booties kept me from feeling it on my feet.

"Don't start that again," Zack said, without even looking. His attention was directed to the walls around us and high above. After hearing so much about the cave and even finding a treasure map that

The Mysterious Treasure

outlined its features, he couldn't believe he was finally here.

"Impressed?" I asked.

"This is the coolest place I've ever been," Zack exclaimed, still gawking. Then turning to us, he shook his fist in the air. "To the ship, you scurvy dogs. We need tools. Shovels, picks, whatever it takes. The wait is over. It's time to unearth our treasure." Zack finished with a flourish, as if he were Jean Laffite himself.

Carrying on about the Leviathan was pointless, so I followed Zack's lead. Taking several deep breaths, the three of us waited for the tide to rush back out. At just the right moment, when the seaweed swayed toward the open sea as if blown by the wind, we launched like torpedoes for the kayak. The swim was easier this time, and soon we were at the mouth of the cave, clearing our snorkels and filling our lungs with air. Once we arrived at the kayak, we lifted our masks from the water, but none of us was prepared for what we saw.

A man and two little girls clung to a capsized rowboat, just fifty feet away. As soon as they saw us, they cried out for help.

Without hesitating, Paige swam for them. I followed, but Zack grabbed my arm.

"What are you doing?" he demanded, his eyes like red embers.

"Going to help."

"We don't have time. The tide's coming in. We've got to find the treasure before it's too late. They've got life vests on. They'll be fine. They can swim to shore."

"Zack, stop being such a jerk. Those girls are scared to death." I twisted free and decided on the one thing that might motivate Zack to help. "Besides, if we don't help them, somebody else will; in fact, lots of boats might come to help. And in the process they'll discover our sea cave."

That did it. Zack quickly climbed into the kayak and pulled the anchor. Joining him there, we paddled over to the boat just as Paige arrived.

"What happened?" I asked.

"It was the weirdest thing," the man gasped. "Something bumped the bottom of our boat. When we leaned over the side to check it out, something flipped us over. It happened right after that sea lion up there started barking."

I glanced up at Bride Rock. "Did you see what bumped you?"

The man tried to catch his breath. "No, not at all."

The girls looked scared to death, so I didn't tell

The Mysterious Treasure

them what I knew it had to be. The slime on the boat confirmed my suspicions.

Paige and Zack set to work to right the capsized boat. Using the kayak, we were finally able to tip it over, but the hull was half full of water. If anyone climbed in, the thing would capsize again.

With no other choice, we agreed to tow them back to the dock. The girls climbed on the center of the kayak. The man and Paige clung to the back of the row boat and kicked. Progress was slow, but after a while we made it.

At the dock, the man thanked us again and again, but it didn't matter to Zack. He just faced the cliffs, his eyes raging. The wind and spray cut at his face, but he hardly blinked. He knew that we couldn't return now. Our arms were limp from exhaustion. And what's worse, the tide had come up, making a swim through the cave impossible.

When Zack finally spoke, it was as much to the ocean as to me and Paige. "Tonight."

"What?" I asked, shooting a sideways glance at Paige.

"Low tide is at eight," Zack told us. "I'll come back then, alone if I have to."

I tried to change his mind. "The wind will be up by then. And what about the big south swell that's supposed to hit?"

"We can make it. The swell's not due until after midnight."

Paige winced in denial. "You seriously want to come at night?"

Zack set his chin. "I will come at night. The swell is supposed to last for at least four days. After that I'm leaving with my parents for vacation. When I get back, who knows how many people will have found that cave."

Remembering my dream from earlier in the week, I started to back away. "Sorry, but—"

"Nate!" Zack shouted, grabbing my shirt. "Don't think about the night, or the waves, or even that stupid serpent. Think treasure! Do you hear me? Treasure!"

Chapter 14

Gram eyed Paige and me suspiciously. "Skin diving at night, huh? What for?"

"Treasure," I laughed, raising my shoulders, as if to make light of the whole thing.

Paige added her two cents. "We could use some of that. Right, Gram?"

Gram pursed her lips and cocked her head. I couldn't believe she was thinking it over. I had expected a "no" right off the bat, and in some ways I would have been relieved. But tonight Gram surprised me. She wrung her hands together, then reached for our chins. When she spoke, her tone was solemn and motherly. "You promise to be careful?"

"We always are," I assured her.

"I know," she said, tears welling in her eyes. "It's just that tonight is such a difficult night for me."

Heebie Jeebies

"Why, Gram?" Paige asked.

I was wondering the same thing. Gram had spent the afternoon preparing for a night out, but the black dress she had on looked more suited for a funeral than a date. If she had any makeup on, it wasn't enough to hide the fear in her face.

"Now, now. Don't you worry yourself about me. I've got some things to take care of this evening, that's all. There's leftovers in the refrigerator you can heat up for dinner. Lock up when you leave, and later tonight we'll have a look at your treasure."

Paige and I glanced at each other in wonder as Gram gathered up her purse and headed out the door. She dabbed her eyes with a tissue as she went.

"What was that all about?" Paige asked.

"I don't know, but it must have to do with money, or our *lack* of it. Why else would she let us go skin diving at night? Even Gram's staking her hope on some lost treasure."

Paige wrinkled her forehead, looking as worried as Gram did when she left.

Three hours later, Paige's worry had turned to fear. And after one look at the ocean, I felt the same way.

The Mysterious Treasure

"If this is low tide, I'd hate to see high tide," I said.

Zack pushed the kayak into the bay. "If we don't hurry up, you will."

We took up the same positions as in the morning. I sat in front. Zack sat in the stern. Paige clung to the back of the boat, kicking her fins intermittently. We could have used her help, but it was more important that she conserve strength for the swim through the sea cave. The shovels and lantern and map remained in the watertight compartments.

"I thought that swell was due *after* midnight," Paige noted.

The ocean heaved and fell, taking us with it.

"Yeah, really. Is this a boat or roller coaster?" I remarked.

"Neither," Zack growled through clenched teeth. "It's a pirate ship. And dead men tell no tales."

I leaned into my paddle, trying to make progress against the liquid hills rolling under us. But it was like trying to scale Mount Everest on a one-speed bike. "Dead is right," I grunted. "If we attempt the sea cave tonight, we will be."

"Mush! You scurvy dogs. Mush!" Zack commanded.

To our right, the faithful sea lion clung to Bride Rock, barking a warning to all who would listen.

"Hear that?" I pointed out. "Something's wrong."

"No way," Zack told me. "He's just jealous of what we will find."

"I doubt it," I muttered to myself, drenched with dread. "I really doubt it."

When we arrived at the sea cave, the situation wasn't as bad as I'd feared. The first ten feet of ceiling remained above water. With a good, strong breath and a wave behind us, traversing the length of the tunnel wouldn't be difficult. Getting back out would be the problem.

As Zack anchored the kayak, I stared up at Old Man Ingram's mansion. No lights were on, making it look even creepier than normal. But I didn't mind. At least if Mr. Ingram was gone, we wouldn't have to worry about him hovering over us like a vulture.

Having secured the kayak, Zack opened the waterproof compartments and divided up the gear. Paige carried the lantern. Zack and I carried the shovels. That left each of us a free hand to hold our dive lights. The map stayed with Zack, in a waterproof container tied to his waist.

We spit in our masks to keep them from fogging, then swam along the top of the water. After exchanging the OK sign, we gulped down several long breaths, then plunged into the sea cave. The

The Mysterious Treasure

water was as cloudy as before, making our flashlights as useless as headlights in the fog. Fortunately we knew the way. With a wave pushing us from behind, we quickly swam the length of the submersed tunnel and surfaced in the cavern.

Zack immediately removed his mask and fins, then started poking around with his shovel. He concentrated on the beach at the end of the cavern.

Standing on her tiptoes, Paige positioned the lantern on a rock and turned it on. Suddenly, the sea cave became a dimly lit room. Seaweed and crabs clung to the rock walls. The ceiling rose above us like a natural bell tower. At thirty feet up, it angled into the cliff out of sight.

"I'd like to know where that goes," I said.

"Some other time," Zack complained. "Now give me a hand, already."

When I applauded, Zack frowned.

"Touchy," I teased. Scanning the ground, I looked for the best place to begin. But a feared and familiar sight distracted me.

"What are you looking at?" Paige asked.

"Guess," I said. I used the shovel to scoop up some of the slime.

"That stuff is so gross," Paige gagged.

"You know what else is gross?" Zack asked, now standing in a two-foot hole. "Drowned teenagers that get stuck in sea caves."

He made his point. I tossed the slime aside and joined the excavation. Scooping out the sand as fast as I could, I quickly got down two feet. But then a wave sloshed in from the tunnel and filled the hole. Determined to keep at it, I splashed out the water and kept digging. Paige poked at the rocks along the base of the cavern, hoping to unearth a trap door.

Zack had the same problem I had with the water, but flung it out faster than it could soak in. "Anything, yet?" he asked, his face red from exertion.

"Not yet," I replied. Another wave squirted past my ankles and filled the hole in front of me. "It's not looking good, Zack. Take out the map so I can see it again."

The map's simple diagram of the sea cave did little to reveal the exact location of the treasure.

I repeated the short poem over and over while scanning the walls and floor.

When the tide is out go in
When the tide is in you win
Your anchor is your treasure.

"That's got to be the stupidest riddle I've ever seen," Zack said.

The Mysterious Treasure

"That's only because you can't solve it," Paige said.

Zack pointed at the "X" on the map, drawn faintly near the back of the sea cave. "This has got to be the treasure. And it's right where we're standing."

"What's weird is that the top of the map is left unfinished."

"That's because they didn't know what's up there anymore than we do. But who cares? Look at the 'X'1. The treasure is down here. When you drop an anchor in the sand, it gets buried. Think about it." Zack thrust his shovel in the sand as fast as a jack hammer.

I was about to do the same, when a look of discovery came over his face.

"I hit something!" he shouted. Dropping to his knees, he burrowed at the sand. "It's a piece of wood."

Joining him, I dug against the tide, moving fast. Our shovels cut through the sand and surf. Finally, he handed me his shovel and worked his arms into the hole to lift his discovery to the surface.

Chapter 15

"Well?" Paige asked.

Straining, Zack lifted and heaved, determined to unearth his find.

"Is it a treasure chest?" I asked.

A moment later I had my answer. Zack lifted a piece of decaying wood to the surface and nothing more.

I dropped my shoulders in despair. "That's it?"

"What do you mean? This tells us we're on the right track." Zack argued, his face as dark as an oil spill.

"More like a *death* track," I said.

A wave surged up through the sea cave, practically knocking me over. Water rose in the cavern up to our knees, before receding again. Zack's mask fell from the stone it had been resting on. I grabbed it just before the backwash could carry it away. I was about to lift it out of the water, when something occurred to me. The lens was blurry.

I brought the mask to my face and looked through the glass. It was blurry like in my dream. "Zack," I said in panic. "What's wrong with your mask?"

"Nothing," he growled. "I had prescription lenses put in. Now get over here and dig, or I'm keeping the treasure for myself."

Suddenly my dream made sense. It wasn't about me at all. The unwillingness to leave, the ceiling holding me down, the Leviathan: it was Zack.

Rushing over, I explained everything to him and Paige. "We've got to get out of here! Now!"

"We're too close," he wailed, pushing me away.

"If we don't leave now, we'll never make it. You want to be stuck in here when the tide comes up and the swell hits? We'll have nowhere to go. We'll either drown or get torn to pieces on these rocks."

"Just a few more minutes," he said, his voice wild with greed.

A wave swirled past our thighs, bumping us into the wall, then pulling us down as it receded.

"You're crazy," I shouted. "Paige, get out of here now. Wait for the backwash, then go."

"I can't make it," she pleaded. "If the water's this

The Mysterious Treasure

high in here, the cave's probably completely submerged on the other side."

"You can make it," I said. "Don't give up. God will help you. Just swim hard, and don't look back."

"What about you?"

"We'll be there soon. Zack has to give up any minute."

Paige donned her mask and fins. With her flashlight to guide her, she stepped to the front of the cavern until only her head was above water. "Nate, I don't want to go alone."

"You can do it," I said.

When she closed her eyes, I knew she was praying. I did the same. Then she took several deep breaths and stuck her snorkel in her mouth. As the backwash withdrew from the cavern, her dive light disappeared into the black water.

I watched the spot where she left, trying to envision how far she was swimming with each second. Ten feet. Twenty feet.

"Keep going, Paige," I cheered, even though she couldn't hear me. "You can make it."

Thirty feet. Forty. Suddenly her light reappeared.

"No!" I cringed.

A burst of water erupted from where Paige descended, followed by her face. She spit out her snorkel and gulped down gallons of air. She tried to stand, but kept tripping on the rocks. A look of horror covered her face.

"What's wrong?" I asked, wading toward her.

"It's the—" Paige stumbled, planting her face in the water.

"The what?" I said, reaching for her.

She surfaced again and pulled off her mask.

"The what?" I repeated, grabbing her hand.

"The Leviathan!" she wailed. "It's back!"

"Where?" I gasped.

"The tunnel! It's coming this—Ahhh!" Paige cried out before disappearing beneath the surface.

I lunged after her and grabbed her hand. Something was pulling her from the other side. All I could think of was the Leviathan's tiny teeth sunk into her flesh. It yanked her toward the tunnel, like a dog pulls on a bone.

I couldn't let go. I held her hand for dear life, and pulled with all my strength. Paige's free foot splashed at the water. Her hand flailed. I screamed for Zack, but he didn't answer. The serpent thrashed near the front of the cavern, then descended.

Wedging my feet against a rock, I pulled with all my might.

All at once, Paige came free. Half-crawling, half-swimming, I dragged her to the back of the cavern.

The Mysterious Treasure

She coughed and clung to the rock wall, petrified of the water. When she lifted her foot I feared the worst, but it wasn't bleeding, just covered with green slime.

"What's going on?" Zack asked.

"Haven't you been listening?" I yelled, ready to go ballistic.

Zack shrugged me off. "I was digging."

"The Leviathan," I seethed through clenched teeth. "It's real. And it's back."

"Yeah right, the Levi—" Zack stopped mid-sentence.

Right in front of us, the Leviathan swam past.

"Now do you believe me?" I shouted.

Without hesitating Zack lifted the shovel over his head. With eyes blazing, he challenged the serpent. "Bring it on, slime-ball! If you think you're getting a piece of my treasure, you're dreaming."

If I didn't know better, I would have thought Blackbeard himself was standing next to me. Following Zack's lead, I raised my shovel over my head. But before either of us could attack, the biggest wave yet erupted from the sea cave and filled the cavern. Saltwater rose to our chests, lifting our feet from the sand. Instinctively, I checked on Paige. She was fine.

But Zack was in trouble. The Leviathan had him by the legs. Zack jabbed at the water, but was soon knocked off his feet.

Chapter 16

Swimming over, I was ready to bring my shovel down like an ax but stopped for fear I'd hit Zack instead of the Leviathan.

As the water receded from the cavern, Zack went with it. A moment later, he was gone.

"Zack!" I screamed out, bounding after him. When my shin slammed against a rock, I fell face first. Instead of climbing to my feet, I searched the tunnel for any sign of Zack or the Leviathan. But the water visibility was terrible.

Making my way to Paige at the end of the sea cave, we searched intently for any sign of Zack.

"Please, God," I prayed. "Help him."

"Nate, do something," Paige cried.

I kicked at the water, feeling helpless. "Please, Lord!" I called out.

Heebie Jeebies

A second later my prayer was answered.

Zack launched from the water like a dolphin. The green monster trailed behind him, along with a massive brown form that I couldn't identify.

Zack splashed toward us, choking on salt water. Wading out to meet him, I rested his arm on my shoulders. Together, we staggered through the waist-deep foam to the back of the cavern.

"Zack, are you all right?" Paige asked, helping support him.

"The sea lion," he choked, gasping for air. "He took on the Leviathan."

Rising to the surface, the sea lion barked as if on fire, then went down again. The next time we saw it, the Leviathan's coils were wrapped around it like a spring.

"Can you see what's happening?," Zack asked, still doubled over.

"Not really," I replied. "And I'm not sure we want to."

"I never even saw its face," Zack admitted. "But its body felt like a python around my legs."

"I saw its face," Paige admitted. "It looked like a moray eel, only ten times as big. It's jaws looked big enough to swallow me whole."

"That sea lion doesn't stand a chance," Zack conceded.

The Mysterious Treasure

"Don't be so sure," I said.

The water exploded in front of us. The sea lion and serpent thrashed above and below the surface. Then as quickly as the fight began it ended. It seemed that we were both right. The serpent had disappeared, and the sea lion floated in the blood-red water, motionless.

"That's the sea lion we saw sitting on the rocks," Paige observed.

Zack shook his head. "Why in the world would he come to save me?"

Before I could respond, the tide brought in another wave, lifting us three feet off the ground, just below where Paige had placed the lantern. The sea lion rose with us, floating just a few feet from our faces.

Our first instinct was to push it away, but after what it had done, we just reached out our hands and gave it a pat. As the surge drained back toward the open ocean, the sea lion went with it.

Soon our feet touched the sand again. Clinging to the rocks, we did our best to maintain our balance.

"This stinks!" Zack shouted. He picked up a shovel and brought it down like an ax, chopping at the water.

"What's your problem?" I asked, backing Paige away from him.

Zack turned to me and blasted. "Try *everything!* That's all! I not only got fooled by a stupid treasure map, I was almost swallowed by a sea monster! The truth is, I'd *be* dead if it wasn't for that sea lion, and now he's dead. What's wrong with me? It's like I'm cursed or something."

"Maybe you are," Paige said.

When Zack looked at me, his eyes groping for an answer, I told him the truth. After everything we'd been through, there was no point in sugar-coating it. "Zack, it's your priorities. They're messed up. You live for worldly stuff instead of God. That's the curse you're under."

Zack didn't answer. He just dropped his shovel and stared.

I continued. "You'd rather go to garage sales than church. You didn't even want to help a shipwrecked family. And you practically shoved Paige off a cliff to get a better look at the sea cave. Those are just a few examples. Believe me, there's more—and God knows every one of them. Why *should* He bless your life?"

That was all Zack needed. Half praying, half crying, he asked God to forgive him. For a moment it looked like he would drop to his knees. But the tide wouldn't allow it.

The Mysterious Treasure

"I need Christ," Zack confessed. "I'm tired of putting it off. I want to believe in Him before it's too late."

I explained the gospel as best I could, that Jesus died on the cross for our sins and rose again, and that forgiveness and eternal life are found only in Him.

Zack nodded in agreement and closed his eyes. What he prayed wasn't neat and organized like you'd hear in a church; but he knew what he was doing, and that's what mattered.

When he opened his eyes, Paige and I were beside him.

"Welcome to the family," Paige said. "And just in time."

"That's for sure," Zack laughed, as another wave swallowed us.

With our situation becoming increasingly grim, the joy of Zack's commitment was hard to sustain. Even with the Leviathan gone, we were anything but safe. The swell had hit, and the tide was rising. It wouldn't be long before the surge from a massive wave burst through the cave and crashed us against the cavern walls.

On the way out, the suction would be impossible to fight. We'd be drawn into the midsection of the sea cave and drowned.

"Our only way is up," Zack said, pointing to a spot twenty feet above us, just below where the tower walls turned into the cliff.

"I'll go for it," I offered. "But these walls are too smooth for climbing."

"And wet," Paige added.

"Looks like we need a miracle," Zack said. "Maybe you two should pray for one."

"Just you saying that is a miracle," I laughed.

"What about the map?" Paige suggested. "Maybe there's something we missed."

"No chance. I've stared at that map for hours. *When the tide is out go in. When the tide is in you win,*" Zack mocked. "What do you win? A trip down the drain?"

"Or up it," I said.

"What are you talking about?" Paige asked.

Before I could explain, the swell brought in another surge, the strongest yet. We rose as if in an aquatic elevator.

On the way up I grabbed the lantern and held it above my head.

We kept rising, ten feet or more. Scraping at the walls, Zack tried to hang on, but couldn't. Sinking back down, our feet never hit the sand. The water was too deep, but we kicked hard and managed to stay clear of the submerged section of sea tunnel.

The Mysterious Treasure

"One more wave, and we're there," I said.

By now Paige and Zack had caught on, and we all waited with anticipation for the next wave. When the surge hit, it might as well have been a geyser. We erupted through the cavern on a bed of frothed foam, ten feet, fifteen, twenty.

"Now," I shouted.

We reached for the ledge and got it!

As the water receded, we hoisted ourselves up. Standing on the thin rock shelf, we pressed our backs against the wall.

"N-now what?" Paige asked, her voice shaking. She tried not to look down.

Turning slowly, I looked for something we could climb on. That's when I saw the bumps on the wall that looked like rings. When I touched them, I realized they were links to a rusty chain.

"Check it out," I said. "It was hidden from below."

Zack's mouth dropped open and he grabbed the chain. "Unreal!"

"You first," I said, sensing his enthusiasm.

But he handed the chain to me. "After that Leviathan thing, I think you better take it. My hands are still shaking."

I yanked on the chain to test its strength, then shimmied for the bend another ten feet above us.

Heebie Jeebies

My hope was that the cavern's tower would become a horizontal tunnel at the top.

It did. But before going any further, I waited for Zack to climb up and hand me the lantern.

"Well?" Paige asked, as she and Zack joined me.

"You won't believe it," I said, holding the lantern in front of me.

At the edge of the lantern's beam, not more than ten feet away, a heavy wooden door with iron hinges marked the end of the tunnel.

Creeping forward, I thought I'd hyperventilate. I couldn't imagine what was in there besides treasure. It had to be.

An antique padlock, covered with rust, secured the latch. Zack held it for a moment, then smashed it loose with a rock.

"Are you ready?" Zack asked, looking at Paige and me.

"Aye, aye, Captain," we said.

With his shoulder against the damp wood, Zack lifted the latch and pushed open the door.

Chapter 17

One look and I wanted to drop the lantern. My hands were trembling like crazy.

"Is that who I think it is?" Zack asked.

Unable to speak, I nodded slowly.

It was my dad, hanging from the wall.

Paige was also too shocked to speak, but she lifted a trembling hand as if to touch him.

"I don't get it," Zack said, stepping all the way into the small stone room. "Why would your dad's picture be hanging here?"

"Beats me," I said, trying to figure out when the picture was taken, and who was in the shot next to him. A few other pictures clung to the stone walls. One had my mom and dad together. Another had people I didn't recognize. Two more had my dad and his friend at different ages, high school probably, and grade school.

Other than the pictures, the rock chamber didn't have much to offer. A box of old diving gear had been left against the wall. A variety of large shells, abalone mostly, covered a shelf. A couple of chairs and a round teak table sat in the center of the room. A few fishing poles leaned in the corner.

The most spectacular item of all was the heavy iron cross buried against the center of the back wall. It was covered with rust, but still beautiful to behold. The peculiar thing was the open loop at the top of the cross. Then a thought occurred to me. I kneeled beside the cross and began to push away the sand from the base. Soon two iron points appeared on each side of it, the same thickness as the cross itself.

"This is it!" I said, excited about my discovery. "Get out the map, quick."

Zack opened the map and I read aloud the last line of the poem, "Your anchor is your treasure."

"I get it," Paige said. "The anchor is a cross. And *that's* our treasure."

"That's so cool," I said, believing my dad had something to do with it. "What do you think, Zack?"

Zack hesitated, stepping toward the cross. "In all honesty, ten minutes ago I would have been disappointed—big time. But the truth is, this is the best treasure I've ever found."

The Mysterious Treasure

"Oh, is it now?" a deep voice boomed from behind us.

We turned slowly around, fearing the worst, which is what we got.

Old Man Ingram stood in the door, his ghostly face ablaze.

"Ahhh!" we screamed, ducking behind the cross.

But not for long.

"Stop that this instant," a woman's voice ordered.

I couldn't believe it. Gram stepped from behind Mr. Ingram into the room. "Stop that screaming, and listen to what Mr. Ingram has to say."

"Gram, what are you doing here?" I gasped.

"Visiting an old friend. Now listen."

"That's all right, Lily," Mr. Ingram said, looking at Gram. "I just wanted these kids to know how important that cross was to their father and my son."

Paige stepped forward, with an amazing sense of calm. "Your son? Is he the one in the picture with my dad?"

"That he is," Mr. Ingram said. "His name was Kirk. He and your dad were best friends growing up. This room was their fortress. They met here to plan adventures, or prepare for voyages. But no matter how many times they went out searching for treasure, they always came back to what mattered most. That old iron anchor, buried to resemble a cross."

"That's nice and everything," Zack said. "But why did you sell me the spyglass for only twenty bucks? And more importantly, why have you been following me?"

"Both questions have the same answer," Mr. Ingram explained. "I wanted you and Nate to find your way here."

"But why'd you wait so long?" I asked. "And Gram, why didn't you ever tell us about this place?"

"I was too angry to talk about it, with you or anyone else."

Old Man Ingram nodded. "Me too, but for different reasons. My son, Kirk, was on the boat the night your parents drowned at sea. In fact, it was my boat, and I was supposed to be on it with them. When they never made it back, I blamed myself."

Gram cleared her throat. "The truth is, I blamed Mr. Ingram too. I felt he should have been on that boat and got them home safe. That's why I told you kids to stay away from this place. But when I learned that the sea cave had reopened, I knew I couldn't put off talking to him any longer."

Mr. Ingram continued. "My wife had died some years earlier, and when I lost my only child, I had no one left. I withdrew into seclusion, from people

The Mysterious Treasure

and the Lord. But after the earthquake opened the sea cave, I knew I couldn't hide any longer. I got my life right with God, then I held a garage sale to reach you kids."

"How'd you know I'd come by?" Zack asked.

Mr. Ingram smiled. "Zack, you're the garage sale baron of Starboard. Even in my isolation, I knew that."

"But Gram," I protested. "What about the tears and the envelope?"

"That had pictures of your father in it that I had never seen. There was also a loan from Mr. Ingram to help repair our house. I was just so grateful—and sorry for the way I had acted."

Mr. Ingram lifted his hands in protest. "Now, there you go again, Lily. I didn't loan you anything. That was a gift."

Gram objected, but continued. "There were other reasons for my tears. Tonight's the ten-year anniversary of the shipwreck. I was also nervous about you finding the cave. Your dad and Kirk never got hurt coming up here, but I still worried."

"They never got hurt?" Zack marveled. "What about the Leviathan?"

"The what?" Gram and Mr. Ingram asked in unison.

Heebie Jeebies

We tried to describe what attacked us and the sea lion's sacrifice on our behalf, but they just looked at us as if we were crazy.

Figuring it was a lost cause, Paige shifted the focus to them. "How'd you two get in here anyway?"

"Secret door," Mr. Ingram said.

"But we never heard you," Paige said.

The old man winked. "If you did, it wouldn't be too secret, now would it?"

"Speaking of secrets," Gram added. "I was the one who scared you away from Mr. Ingram's last night. I couldn't resist having a little fun."

Just outside the wooden door, Mr. Ingram showed us a spot in the wall where the rock swung open. We followed him through the secret passage, up a flight of stairs, to the cellar of his house. From there, we strolled out back to check on Zack's kayak and enjoy the view from the cliff.

What a sight it was. The dreary weather was gone. The sky had finally cleared. The moon's reflection ran across the sea like a trail of ivory paint. Stars bloomed above us in a garden of light. Zack's kayak remained in place, held secure by the anchor, even as the thick waves rolled by.

Then a triumphant bark rose from the water below.

THE MYSTERIOUS TREASURE

"Check it out," Zack said. He stepped between Paige and me and put his arms on our shoulders. "He's alive."

I stared down at the ocean and beamed. The sea lion had regained his throne on top of Bride Rock. And even in the darkness, we could sense his majestic eyes watching over us all.

Epilogue

Mr. Ingram turned out to be a great guy, and the following spring he and Gram were married. After their honeymoon, we all moved into the mansion above the cliffs. My room is upstairs, with an incredible view of the ocean.

Zack and I turned the stone room above the sea cave into our captain's quarters. Zack brought over a lot of his nautical antiques for decorations, giving the room an authentic look. The iron cross is still there. Zack wouldn't have it any other way. His faith in Christ is as deep as the sea.

The sea monster never did show up again, and to this day what it was remains a mystery. Zack believes it was the world's largest moray eel. He attributes the slime in the cavern to anemones. As for the green ooze around our house, Paige came up with a snail and slug theory, based on the heavy rain at the time. For me, there's only one explanation: it was Leviathan, just like the Bible describes.

The sea lion, on the other hand, is still with us, enthroned on Bride Rock. Whenever we go for a dive, we see him basking in the sun and watching us closely, just to make sure we're OK.

The spyglass that Ingram sold Zack was just one of many he owns. He began collecting them when Kirk and my parents disappeared at sea. Sometimes when I'm feeling lonely, I go into the den and take one down from the wall. From there I go to the back deck and make myself comfortable.

On occasion, Mr. Ingram grabs a spyglass and joins me. We search across the water, watching the seagulls and swells and the dolphins bursting through the whitecaps. But most of all we watch the blue horizon, hoping to see a lost sailboat miraculously appear.

In my dream Kirk is at the helm, and Mom and Dad are beside him. Blown off course, and given up for dead, they've managed to find their way home after all these years.

Like I said, it's just a dream. But I can't help wishing it were true. Every day I think about my mom and dad, how difficult it is to grow up without them.

The Mysterious Treasure

But the Lord helps me, and I know my parents don't have to come back for me to see them again. One day, somewhere between the ocean and sky, I'll sail out to meet them . . . in paradise with God.

Don't miss another exciting

HEEBIE JEEBIES

adventure!

Check out a chapter from

UNCLE FROM ANOTHER PLANET

Chapter 7

I don't know what woke me up. All I know is that I looked around in the dark, strange room and groaned when I remembered where I was. I was lying on top of the covers because it was so hot without any windows open. I'd been dreaming that I was at home with Mom, Dad, and Dylan and we were getting ready to eat dinner. But now, awake, everything that had happened that day came flooding back. I was not a happy camper.

I lay on my back and put my hands behind my head. I knew it would be hard to get back to sleep because of the heat. I was tempted to get up and pry open the glass door to the balcony for some fresh air—but I couldn't bring myself to do it. Uncle Allen scared me. I *had* to do what he said—even though he'd never know if I opened a window or not.

I tried to relax. It would only be a week, I reminded myself. Just six more nights of sleeping in this bed and I'd be back home where I belonged.

I stared up at the ceiling, trying to give myself a pep talk. You'll have fun, I told myself. You'll explore the farm. You'll have a great time with Jeremy and Angie—and once you get to know Uncle Allen, he won't seem so weird. Everything will look better in the light of day.

Just then, I noticed some faint lights shimmer across the ceiling—like the ones that crossed my bedroom ceiling back home when a car passed, late at night, on the street outside my window. But out here we were about a half mile from the nearest highway.

It occurred to me that maybe someone was coming up the grassy driveway to the house. For a few seconds I entertained the notion that maybe Mom had come back to get us and was now pulling up outside the house—but I knew that wasn't very likely. And my room was on the side of the house, not the front. The lights couldn't be from the driveway.

I stared at the ceiling for a few minutes, but the lights were gone. I looked around the room. Maybe it was a reflection, but there was hardly anything in

Uncle From Another Planet

the room, and what was there was coated with dust—none of it could make a reflection.

I had just about decided it was all in my imagination, when I looked back at the ceiling and saw the light skim across it again. I was spooked, and I wished I hadn't picked a room so far away from Jeremy and Angie.

I got out of bed and tiptoed to the glass door. The glass was streaked with dust, but I could still see through it. I cupped my hands against the glass and looked out. It was nothing like the night sky at home, where I can sometimes make out the Big Dipper and not a whole lot more.

The land and all the trees near the house were black, and above them stretched a dome of shimmering bright lights. I could clearly see the faint white streak of the Milky Way stretched like a ragged ribbon over the dark farmland. The sky was sparkling and lonely, like when you stand on a dark hill and look down on the city at night. It was beautiful in an eerie kind of way. I felt a lump begin to grow in my throat again, when I thought about how far away my family was.

As I stood staring into the darkness, something strange and impossible happened. Three bright lights suddenly streaked upward out of the fields on the other side of the trees across the yard. They formed a perfect triangle, without a sound, about a hundred yards away from where I was standing.

I was so shocked, I felt like something had hit me in the chest—I stumbled backward and sat down on the bed. *What in the world was that?* I asked myself. I tried to keep it out of my mind, but all I could think of was the last picture Dylan drew for me—the one where Jeremy, Angie and I were being taken away in a triangular flying saucer. My heart began jackhammering in my chest. *No,* I told myself. *It's impossible.*

I crept back to the glass door and peeked out. The night sky was back to normal. Whatever it was that had rocketed up out of the field on the other side of Uncle Allen's trees was gone. It was probably miles away by now—at least I hoped it was.

More exciting releases from HEEBIE JEEBIES

THE NEW QUICK-READING TALES THAT ENTERTAIN WHILE AFFIRMING THE PRESENCE AND POWER OF GOD!

It's thrills and chills of the unexpected kind when Ryan, Jeremy, and Angie spend a week at old Uncle Allen's farm. Ryan is convinced that their hermit uncle is really an alien who has come to take the three of them to some strange planet.

Uncle from Another Planet   0-8054-1650-1

available at fine bookstores everywhere

More exciting releases from

HEEBIE JEEBIES

THE NEW QUICK-READING TALES THAT ENTERTAIN WHILE AFFIRMING THE PRESENCE AND POWER OF GOD!

In this eerie tale filled with unexpected thrills and chills, Heather and Todd pursue an investigation to learn about a mysterious abandoned camp, their father's own secret involvement, and God's all-powerful protection and love.

Welcome to Camp Creeps
0-8054-1195-X

Twelve-year-old Daniel finds himself face-to-face with a ten-foot-long rat and his own guilty conscience in the first edition of the spine-chilling *Heebie Jeebies* series. Will Daniel learn that covering up a mistake can be the biggest mistake of all?

The Rat That Ate Poodles
0-8054-0170-9

available at fine bookstores everywhere